TRIGGER SWITCH

BOOKS BY BRYON QUERTERMOUS

The Dominick Prince Series
Murder Boy
Riot Load
Trigger Switch

BRYON QUERTERMOUS

TRIGGER SWITCH

ALL
DUE
RESPECT

All Due Respect Books
an imprint of Down & Out Books
3959 Van Dyke Road, Suite 265
Lutz, FL 33558
DownAndOutBooks.com

Cover design by JT Lindroos

ISBN: 1-64396-190-X
ISBN-13: 978-1-64396-190-3

For Dan Malmon, friend, brother,
sounding board and arch-nemesis

Chapter One

I met Dutchy Kent at a bar in Long Island City an hour after I flew in from Detroit. It was nasty, the kind of place I didn't know even existed anywhere in the twenty-first century anymore, let alone somewhere as overpriced as New York City. He led me into a narrow wood paneled alley where two people could barely stand next to each other facing the back wall. We took the two seats at the end furthest from the door and ordered beer. I half expected to see the bartender draw our drinks from a tap with a generic black and white handle that just said BEER.

Instead, he opened two cans of PBR, poured them into mason jars, and slid them down to us. It didn't take long after that to realize we were in a hipster bar and it looked like this on purpose. I took a long gulp of the beer and enjoyed the ironic flavor until Dutchy gave the bartender a twenty and didn't get any change back.

I'd been to shitty bars around Detroit where that could have bought an entire round. Not these days. And not downtown anymore. But a few years ago someplace like Taylor or Melvindale where they still had guys who worked in the auto plants making okay money. What the hell did anyone do around here that they could pay ten dollars for a beer but had to live in a shitty apartment building on a street that smelled like toasted garbage and electric pee?

Dutchy sucked his beer down in one long gulp and ordered another. And a shot of whiskey. And a cheeseburger. He never asked if I wanted anything. I never wondered what I would have said if he had asked. I just sipped my beer and waited for Dutchy to say something to make this all worthwhile.

Dutchy had been an asshole to me in high school, as he was to most of us in the class who didn't quite know what to make of someone appearing on our televisions Saturday mornings and then showing up for homeroom on Monday. But by college his brief career as a child star had come to an end and we'd bonded over pulp novels and our disdain for the rest of our classmates. We maintained something of a friendship, even though he had a nasty temper, a penchant for mean-spirited—and often dangerous—practical jokes, and the tendency to get us both into heaps of trouble. We lost touch over the years until our relationship was reignited over the internet. He'd read my first novel and loved it and emailed me to find out if it was really me, because he never believed I had any talent. We emailed back and forth, became Facebook friends briefly, and then a week ago he'd emailed me a script based on one of my published short stories. He said he wanted to put it on in New York City to help revive his acting career.

The whole thing sounded too much like one of his epic shitstorms, but I was desperate to get out of Detroit, out of Michigan, and away from my ex-wife's family who claimed they didn't hold a grudge for me murdering her, but I wasn't exactly sold on their change of heart.

"It's been ages, man," he finally said. "I can't believe we're still here. You know?"

"Still alive you mean?"

"Still *alive*, man," he said, pushing the plate away from him. "Alive in the spirit. Alive in the arts. Alive in our *dreams*."

"Oh, right. I guess."

"Look around, man. Look at the saps out there going to a job. Cashing a check. Riding the train. Living their bullshit."

"Ten-dollar beers, man," I said, holding my mason jar high. "Gotta do something to keep 'em coming."

"I don't know. It all seems so…I just don't know man. I couldn't do it."

I nodded and bit my tongue. I didn't want to argue. I just wanted another beer and a sign that things weren't as shitty as I suspected they were.

"Which makes this all even harder," Dutchy continued.

"All what?"

He pushed the rest of his dishes down the bar so there was nothing in front of him but a wet napkin. He balled the napkin up in his hand and held it out to me.

"All of this."

"Is this a metaphor?"

"It's a reality. It's all we have left."

"You gotta give me a little more here. I'm not—"

"We're busted. Broke. Done."

"The show?"

"The theater. All of it."

"Well shit," I said. "That would have been good to

know before now."

"Probably."

He looked away from me and stared down the other end of the bar for a while.

"So what are we going to do?" I asked. "My flight doesn't leave for another week and I don't have the money to change it."

"I do have some ideas."

The way he said it, the tone, put me off. It wasn't right. It was planned. It was rehearsed. He was playing me. I waited for him to keep talking. I wanted to see how far he was willing to go.

"Are you in?"

I nodded, sort of. I still didn't say anything though. So he kept talking. I used to have a problem keeping my mouth shut, and it never failed to come back around and kick me in the ass. Dutchy rambled for almost half an hour before he said something that made sense.

"There's some money," he said. "Some money that went missing from the theater that I've been looking for. If we can find that, and I'm close, I just need a...I need a partner, someone with some life experience in this stuff, if you know what I mean, but if we can find this cash, we'll be set up right."

"This is bullshit," I said. "I'm out."

"That's no way to look at this," he said, putting his hand on my shoulder. "You're missing the opportunity in it all. The chance to—"

I shrugged his hand off my shoulder and stood up. "You're an asshole. You dragged me all the way out here under this bullshit notion of my New York theater debut but all you really need is a stooge."

"This isn't just about you, Dominick. This is about

4

me. We're both on our last outs here and I don't have anybody else I can bring in from the bench."

"I'm sure you think you're tapping into an emotional vein with that baseball talk," I said. "What with you and me being old college buddies and such, right?"

"It's the truth, man."

"The truth," I said, squatting down to his eye level and leaning in as close as I could to his face without touching it, "is that the last guy I buddied up with was a serial killer who murdered at least three people before my ex-wife blew him away in an alley. So excuse me if I don't tear up at your fucking nostalgia trip and jump headfirst into this stupid scheme that is likely to get both of us killed."

"I—"

"I needed an escape," I said. "And you fucked that up."

I left the bar with the cockiest and toughest swagger I could muster and made it two blocks toward my hotel before I collapsed into a heap on the sidewalk and started crying. Nobody paid me any attention and I was able to work out my shit in relative peace before trying to figure out what my next move would be.

The first step was to get back to my hotel room where I had a lock, a television, a hot shower, and a bed. I stripped to my underwear and got under the covers and passed out. When I woke up, Judge Judy was yelling at someone about being responsible for what her son did in their neighbor's yard. I didn't feel great, but I felt rested, something I hadn't felt in a very long time.

Between the nightmares and flashbacks of the violence I'd seen the last couple of years—and the brand new fear of my in-laws coming to whack me—sleep had been rare and fitful at best. But in a new city, a city of millions of people that made it easy to hide, I slept like a drugged lab monkey. A long hot shower finished off the revitalization, and by the time I flopped onto the bed again, this time as Dr. Oz was leading a group of overweight housewives through a comically large digestive system set, I felt a flicker of optimism. A flicker bright enough to grab the tourism guide off the desk next to the bed and flip through it looking for something to do. Something in the city.

The real New York City.

I skipped down the steps, out of the hotel, and up the two blocks and over the one block to the Queensboro Plaza subway station. It felt weird calling it the subway because I had to climb two flights of stairs and cross the street to get to the platform, but once I was near the tracks, everything looked like it did in the movies. It was loud and weirdly cold and smelled like oil and garbage. The mix of people standing around waiting for the next train was staggering in its diversity. I made my way over to the big map of the subway lines and after a few disorienting moments, I figured out where I was going. When the 7 train pulled into the station, I jumped on with everyone else and waited for my adventure to begin.

There was far more wobbling and screeching than I would have expected and soon we were plunged underground into darkness with the train speeding up and slowing down at random intervals. I listened, fascinated, as the automated voice over the loudspeaker announced stop after stop. Subtle is not my natural state of being but I tried very hard not to stare as I ran my eyes up and down the seats evaluating my fellow riders. There were more families than I expected and more normal-looking people. I had assumed everyone would be fabulous and vaguely famous, but there were enough frumpy and goofy-looking people that made me feel at home. They all looked so natural on the train though, and I tried to be natural but was too aware of myself. So I embraced my tourist self, hoping my luck wasn't rotten enough to get mugged twice in one day. It wouldn't have mattered anyway though, because when I finally emerged from the subway up through the Times Square/42nd Street station into the magical bubble of lights and sound and electricity that made up the crossroads of the world, any hope I had of looking natural blew away.

And I could not have cared less. It was amazing. I slowly spun around with my head tilted as far back as it would go, trying to absorb as much of it as possible as quickly as possible. I could feel the renewal like my spirit had been waiting for this moment my entire life. I briefly felt validated in all my efforts, good, bad, or inexplicable, to get to that city and wondered if maybe there was a chance my life could turn out right. In fact, I felt so good that I expected a thunderstorm to pop up or someone to stick a gun in my ribs. But the worst that happened was I was jostled around by a pack of tourists just like me whose necks didn't go as far back as mine did.

And then I saw Elmo doing the electric slide with Iron Man and I felt even better. I finally stopped spinning and made my way to the bright red set of bleachers smack dab in the middle of the street to see what that was all about. I climbed to the top of the narrow bleachers and found myself with an even better view of the whole area. My body was vibrating as I tried to decide what to do next. There were all the restaurant chains and store chains we had at malls back home but that seemed like a waste of the energy of Times Square. I was hungry again and thought about getting something from one of the food carts, but I was paralyzed by excitement and couldn't move so I stared for a while longer. When my senses were so overloaded that they blew me back to reality, I exited the bleachers to go and see what was around back.

I was in New York City for my stage debut but the truth was I had never seen a play before—well, nothing beyond the odd community theater massacre of Rodgers and Hammerstein—and I figured it was about time. My budget was limited so I couldn't afford any of the big ticket shows but while I was staring at the big electronic board listing all of the shows waiting for a sign, someone handed me a flyer for a play called *Perfect Crime* offering tickets for twenty-five dollars. I bought a ticket for the two p.m. matinee that started in fifteen minutes, watched the show, and halfway through figured out what I was going to do with Dutchy.

The play was awful, but I loved the experience. The theater was a few blocks up from the TKTS booth across from another giant Applebee's and next to a closed strip club called Bare Essence and an open sex toy store called Mixed Emotion. I was disappointed by the lack of imagination in the naming but excited to be in one of the last vestiges of Times Square's grimy peep show era that had been immortalized in my mind from too many viewings of *Taxi Driver* and *NYPD Blue*. There was a group of us standing just outside of the theater waiting to be called back in after the intermission was over. Some were smoking, some were analyzing the clues from the play, and a few of us were fidgeting, wondering how best to walk away without looking rude. One of them was a girl I guessed to be about my age dressed casually, not like part of the theater crowd. We'd made eye contact a few times before the show started. The front row of the theater, where all the discount ticket holders were put, had the feeling of a freshman campus mixer because we were bonded together and different from the rest of the folks around us. When she caught my gaze again, she came over to me.

"New York Fucking City," she said, waving her hand in the air.

"Aren't you New Yorkers all supposed to be jaded and cynical?"

"I'm from Michigan. Just moved here last week to be a writer."

"Huh," I said.

A year ago I would have been jealous of her. I would have rambled endlessly about my own Michigan background and my own writing dreams and my own writing projects. But right then I just hoped to god she wouldn't ask me where I was from and what I was doing in the city. Lucky for me she seemed content to continue talking about herself.

"I work at a different theater, over in Brooklyn, doing accounting work believe it or not. I know that may seem like a silly job for a writer, but I'm good with numbers and who wants to be another cog at some shitty online magazine or get coffee for some bullshit publisher in Brooklyn, right?"

"Yeah. Sure. I get it," I said.

I waited until the office manager called us back in and broke off from the crowd right before entering, but as I turned, I saw the girl I'd been talking to following me.

"Hey, I'm Bianca," she said, holding her hand out as she sped up her pace to catch up with me. "You're not one of the regulars here are you?"

"Regulars?"

I stopped walking, but she continued toward me tripping on the sidewalk and falling into me so hard she knocked us both into the wall. As she pushed off of me, her mouth was close enough to my face that I could smell wintergreen gum on her breath. Her hands pushed off of my waist and crotch in a way that I was almost certain was supposed to be seductive, but before I could respond, she had been absorbed by a passing crowd and I headed back toward Times Square, confused and exhilarated.

There was so much more I wanted to look at and to experience, but the first half of the play and my conversation with Dutchy had shaken loose my devious side, and I wanted to get to work. Just as I reached the subway station to head back to Queens, it started pouring rain and I noticed my phone and my wallet were gone. I rushed back to the theater to see if they'd fallen out of my pocket during the show, but that seemed silly. My wallet had been in my back pocket despite my mother's paranoid warning before I left, and I would never, ever, live that down. In her long and rambling pre-trip lecture she had recommended I keep my wallet in my front pocket so no one could pickpocket me and that I keep my wad of emergency cash in my shoe because muggers never ask anyone to take off their shoes to check for money.

It was still raining when I got off the train. I remembered seeing a cyber café nearby and was able to find the place just before the rain soaked me completely through. I gave the cashier a five-dollar bill from my sock emergency fund in exchange for three hours of internet access and thought I might have overpaid until I realized how slow the computers were and that it could take the entire three hours for me to log into my email.

I could have logged into my Apple account to get the full picture of where my phone was, but that site was slow to load on my good computer, so I went with the simplest option and logged into Gmail. I had three emails waiting for me from my phone. The last location logged had been a block from where I was at the theater at almost the same time I'd been there. Either I was in a weird romantic comedy and this was part of our meet-cute, or whoever stole my phone was following me. I immediately thought of the woman who bumped into me outside of the theater.

I sat back and folded my arms behind my head in a very dramatic thinking gesture wondering how to play this. A new move presented itself though when an email came in from my phone. The location logged was the café where I was sitting.

Chapter Two

There were only a handful of people in the café, maybe a dozen or so, but it was a small, narrow dungeon beneath a dry cleaner with no windows to the outside and few white faces. I felt like a spy, or an innocent man on the run, trying to ignore the fact I was really just a dumb and lost tourist. Nobody made eye contact with me, so I tried to shake something loose and struck up a conversation with the lanky Asian person of indeterminate gender behind the counter.

"I think somebody here might have my phone," I said, softly.

"No phones. Outside," they said in androgynously modulated tone, pointing to a sign on the wall, one of several I was just noticing, that said NO PHONES with a comically aggressive red line drawn through a clip art cell phone of early 1990s vintage.

"No, I don't want to talk, I think some—"

"Shhhhhhhh," they said. "Outside."

I wasn't going to get any further down that path, so I sat back down and logged out of the computer, waiting for a better idea to hit me. Nothing jumped out as particularly brilliant and I moped for a few paces back toward the hotel before realizing I didn't need to do anything at all if I didn't want to. Well, at least nothing more than paying closer attention to my surroundings. I was beginning to suspect my robbery had not been random and whoever had my phone was teasing me—likely at the behest of Dutchy—but I suspected whoever it was would eventually make contact with me and we could get on with whatever was going on. I was mostly confident that didn't involve killing me, but not entirely, hence the better attention to my surroundings. In the meantime, I would focus on figuring out what kind of crap Dutchy was trying to drag me into.

Back at the hotel, the clerk on duty waved me over and handed me a slip of paper with a phone number on it.

"Your friend Dutchy left a note to have you call him when you returned."

"He's not my friend," I said quickly. "He's an old classmate. He wants me to do something with him and…"

"Yes, sir?"

"It's complicated."

"I know people like that."

"This thing we're working on," I said, "it could be cool, but I have some reservations."

"Because of who he is?"

I nodded. "You know who he is?"

"I loved *Home Room* when it was on," he said. "My very first crush was—"

"Robin Jo Brandy. Me too. Anyway, you probably know about this theater thing he has going—"

"Of course," he said, clapping his hands in my face. "You're the writer."

That was the first time anyone had referred to me

that way and I didn't know how to unpack it. Part of it was intoxicating, part of it was unnerving, and part of it was just plain depressing. I hadn't written anything in more than a year and hadn't even thought about writing anything in more than six months. Even the script for the play Dutchy wanted to put on, though based on a story I wrote, had been written by someone other than me.

"Yes," I said. "The writer. How did you know?"

"It's probably a cliché, you know, this being New York City and all, but I always wanted to be a writer."

"No, I mean, how did you know about the project? About Dutchy?"

"New York City might be a big city, but this little burg we got here is like a small town and this fine hotel is the town square. Everybody knows everybody's business, especially Dutchy's business 'cause he can't seem to keep his mouth shut about anything."

"That's cool. City this big I'm sure there's lots of people trying to be lots of things. What do you write?"

"Little bit of everything, I guess. Started with plays when I first moved here, but didn't get anywhere with that so I tried novels. Now I'm pursuing my dream of hotel management."

"Oh," I said. "Well..."

"I'm kidding," he said. "I wrote a few action novels in the eighties and I ghostwrite teen horror novels and CEO biographies now."

"Oh," I said.

"It's good money. But I got a kid and, believe it or not, the benefits here are pretty good and I normally work the midnight shift, so I have plenty of time to write."

"So hey, you seem to know the area, and know the players, and kind of know what's...up, you know?"

He narrowed his eyes and leaned away from me. "I guess…"

I'd lost his goodwill and didn't think he'd do a favor for me now just out of the goodness of his heart or as part of his broad customer service responsibility.

"I know you probably don't need the money, but—"

"You heard I had a kid, right?"

I laughed awkwardly; he laughed desperately.

"Anyway," I said. "I need your help."

"With Dutchy's thing?"

"You in?"

"I'm off in an hour."

I nodded, like I was thinking through something important. An hour was a long time considering how much had happened since I got off the plane that morning. But I also couldn't do this alone.

"Do you, like, live here or something?" I asked. "Do you need to change clothes or something?"

"I usually go to the gym after work so I've got other clothes. Should we meet somewhere so people don't see us leaving together?"

"I don't think that'll be a problem," I said. "People aren't usually surprised when they see me getting extra help from people."

"Putting on an act, right? Act simple so people don't look at you too hard when the complicated shit goes down?"

"An act. Right."

The clerk was off exactly an hour after I left the desk and he shook my hand and said, "You can call me Billy."

"I need to do some spying," I told him, "and I kind

of suck at hiding in the shadows."

"Spying on Dutchy?"

"He's a complicated guy, you know? I need to make sure that what he's told me holds up before I decide to stick around or not."

"Sure, sure. I get it. We live in complicated times, can't trust anyone, all of that. I got it."

"Great, cool. Okay then," I said. "So what would be really great is if you had access to a car."

"We have an old Town Car the hotel uses to take people back and forth to the airport. The guy who drives it during the day owes me a favor, so if you don't care about getting diverted if a fare calls, he should be good."

As we sat on a bench outside the hotel waiting for the car to arrive, I realized this guy could be another yahoo trying to set me up. But I'd told him my story, he knew I was broke, so why would he try to rob me?

Shit. I wasn't broke. I actually had money in my account and I could hit up a bank to get a new debit card. It was after six, so I guessed most of the Bank of America branches in the area were closed. I instinctively reached for my phone to send a note to myself as a reminder and was disappointed once again to find it wasn't there. Every time I saw something I wanted to take a picture of, every time I had a random thought I wanted to check through Google, and every time I wanted to check my email to see if any kind of amazing writing opportunity had come my way.

Like Dutchy wanting to do my play.

Something was firing in my brain, but I wasn't making any connections yet. I scratched the top of my palm, trying to focus my thoughts to see what was brewing, but we were interrupted by the arrival of the Town Car.

Billy the hotel clerk was first off the bench to the car and stopped me before I got in.

"You don't have to call shotgun or anything," I told him. "You can sit in the front if you want."

"Bizzy is a tough nut, emotionally," he said. "So don't be a chatty passenger."

"I'm not a fucking lunatic, asshole," Bizzy said, popping his thick, hairy head up through the moon roof to look at us. "This guy acts like I'm some kind of special flower because I don't write trash for money like he does."

Another fire. Another thought. But still…nothing yet.

As I got into the back seat, Billy climbed into the front seat and explained who I was and what I was looking for. I stared in awe at how big of a man Bizzy was. He was soft and beefy with broad shoulders and a broad, jiggly chest. He had hair everywhere and wheezed like a squeak toy on its way to the trash heap. When he spoke again, his voice boomed and rolled off the soft leather interior of the car.

"Car full of writers," he said. "Better hope we don't run outta gas, right?"

"I can pay you for your time," I said. "I need to get to a bank tomorrow when they open to—"

"Didn't mean money, asshole. Look at all of us with our pretty hands and pasty faces. Nobody in this car is gonna want to smell like a gas pump."

"Ah, right," I said.

"This guy," Bizzy said to Billy, shaking his thumb in my direction. Billy shrugged.

I slumped down into my seat and watched while we wound through the neighborhood. Billy didn't know where I wanted to go, but I was curious to see where he would take me. When we drove past a strip of business with a marquee sign at the end of the block, all the random firing thoughts in my head hit a trip wire at once.

"She's a writer too," I said out loud without any context. "I bet you know her?"

Bizzy looked at Billy again, confused and irritated.

"Who do we know?" Billy asked.

"The bitch who robbed me. When she was talking to me, I don't think she was faking. She talked about being a writer and not wanting to be a cog in a magazine and a bunch of other crap I've said almost verbatim myself."

"The fuck makes you think we would know anyone who would rob you?" Bizzy asked.

"Oh, shit, no offense or anything," I said. "It's just that you guys are both writers in this area and I bet she's from here and I bet Dutchy talked her into doing this as some kind of bullshit prank."

Billy was nodding his head as I spoke. "He did seem like an asshole."

"I wish I had my email," I said. "I think I've got her name in there somewhere."

"You could describe her, maybe we recognize her or something," Bizzy said.

"I never saw a picture of her though. Dutchy just kind of dropped her name once and I thought it sounded important so I—"

"I think he means to describe the driver who jacked you," Billy said. "See if maybe we recognize her as a writer we know."

"Sure, right. Yeah. That makes sense. I mean she was sitting down so I don't know how tall she was, but her legs weren't up to her chin or anything, so maybe average height."

"Maybe something about how she looks. You're a writer, right?"

"Right. Yes. She looked like me, honestly. I mean not like twins or anything, but she looked like she was from Michigan, or somewhere like that. Not a native, I mean. She said she was from Iowa and I wonder if maybe that's the truth."

"Best way to lie is to base it in truth," Bizzy said.

"Right. I mean do you guys even know anybody who writes plays or anything like that? Screenplays maybe, I bet there's some overlap."

"That's no brilliant description or anything," Bizzy said. "But it sure does sound like Bianca."

"Goddammit she even used her real name," I said. "I'm such a moron."

Billy kept on nodding his head. "I don't think you'll get any argument on that from up here," he said. "But what do we do next?"

"Do you know where she is? Can we find her? I want to find her."

Bizzy slammed on the brakes and I flew forward, almost completely into the front seat. He turned around and grabbed my face in his meaty, hairy hands.

"You stay the fuck away from Bianca Dade, you hear?"

"Um…"

"He's right," Billy said. "That's some messy shit."

"Well I know she's crazy. She fucking robbed me."

"It's not just her though. It's Teddy."

"Who's Teddy? Is that her boyfriend?"

"Nobody fucking knows. But he's a lunatic and so is she and just stay the fuck away from them."

"I think she wrote the play Dutchy is doing," I said.

"Based on *my* story."

"Get outta my car."

"What? No way. I need—"

"Yeah, it's probably best if you get out," Billy said. "I can close out your bill out at the hotel and suggest somewhere else that—"

"No. No way," I said. "I need your help."

"You need to get the fuck outta town is what you need."

"My flight doesn't leave for another week and I can't afford to change it."

"The hotel has some pull at the airlines. I bet we could get it knocked down enough for you to make it—"

"What is happening here? What did I do?"

Neither of them spoke for a very long stretch of seconds and they wouldn't even make eye contact with each other.

Finally, Billy said, "You've incurred the wrath of one of the nastiest drug dealers in Queens and when he murders you we don't want to be around as collateral damage."

Chapter Three

I watched sadly as another car drove away from me in Queens. Rather than being pissed this time though, I was confused. Confused and a little bit scared. But I was just a block away from the theater where Dutchy had claimed all my dreams would come true, so I did what I've always done when I don't know what else to do: I pushed forward and hoped to luck into something good or die quickly.

If not for the shiny new marquee announcing a new show was coming soon, the Tate Theater could easily be mistaken for a liquor store. There was a giant rolling metal gate pulled down over the doorway and a batch of graffiti looked to have been recently painted over. I shook the gate, wondering if that was how you made it known that you wanted to get in, but nothing happened. I looked at the two business next to it and thought about going in and doing some reconnaissance first, but I was eager for results, so I went around to the side of the building to look for another door. I found a big metal door with no handle toward the middle of the building under a small plaque that said "Stage Door." I banged on the door mercilessly until someone opened it.

"I need to see Dutchy," I said, trying to wedge my body into the doorway.

"The bookstore down the block will let you people use the bathroom. You don't need to—"

"My name is Dominick Prince and Dutchy brought me here."

The door didn't open any further, but whoever was on the other side of it stopped pushing me away so hard.

"Dutchy don't bring nobody here."

The door opened a little more and I saw a skinny white kid with bad hair and pockmarked skin wearing a yellow jumpsuit. He looked like a hip hop background dancer from the nineties. He also looked a lot easier to intimidate than I had initially imagined so I threw my entire weight into pushing him out of the way. When he fell too easily and landed on his back, I took the opportunity to jump on top of him and whale on him, letting the entire morning's worth of anger and fear and confusion out on this poor guy with the nerve to be helpful and open the door, until someone grabbed me from behind and pulled me off him.

"Jesus Christ," Dutchy said. "Where did *that* come from?"

I kept swinging and kicking and landed a couple of lucky hits on Dutchy's gut and knees so he dropped me. I punched him in the face again, but this time it hurt me more and he didn't fall down.

"Tell me about Bianca Dade."

"I don't know what you're talking about."

I went to punch him again, but he caught my hand and used some kind of martial arts move to twist my hand and push the energy from the punch back at me, sending me flailing into the wall behind me.

"She wrote the script for my story. The one you brought me out here to stage."

"I hate to ruin whatever this is you've got going on in your head buddy, but *I* wrote that script."

"No," I said. "Billy and Bizzy said her name was Bianca and that—"

"Who the fuck are Billy and Bizzy? Your balls?"

My brain was slowing down and I had less confidence in my motivation. Paranoia had always been a problem with me—though not entirely without reason, FYI—and second guessing was second nature, so I had to wonder if I was blowing all of this out of proportion.

"We were talking once," I said. "You and I, about the script, and you mentioned a girl who was involved. I know it was a girl. It sounded important so I—"

"Jesus, man, I think you broke my kneecap," Dutchy said. "That really hurt."

"Can we go somewhere and talk? Do you have an office here or something? Like, away from...everyone else."

"We can go sit on the stage, nobody will bother us in there."

I followed Dutchy down a dark hallway to my left that led us out to a small lobby and then through the lobby doors into the performance area. Unlike the theater where I'd seen *The Perfect Crime,* which only had seats in front of the stage, this theater had seats on three sides that were very close to the black wood stage. There were two folding chairs and two black music stands on the stage. Dutchy sat down in the chair furthest away from me and I sat down next to him.

"Is it going to be a musical?" I asked, wiggling the

music stand in front of me.

"We seem to be on different pages with this whole thing, you and I."

"Because you're a slimy son of a bitch who brought me here to be your stooge and I won't go along with it?"

"That hurts."

"I can punch you again, see which hurts more."

Dutchy pushed the music stand in front of him away and turned his chair so he was facing me.

"We obviously don't have a sterling history together, and I'm certainly aware that my behavior when I was younger left much to be desired, but I was hoping we'd finally found something we can share that we can build on and start over."

"Okay," I said, turning my chair in the same way he'd turned his so we were facing each other. "Just tell me one thing: why me?"

"You certainly don't sound very grateful for an opportunity that most writers would beg for."

It was clear I was in over my head and had no business being involved in any way with Dutchy. So for once in my life, I walked away.

And Dutchy hit me in the back with the fucking music stand.

It hurt, a lot, but didn't knock me to the ground. I turned around and he hit me again, this time in the legs. That did knock me down and when he wound up to hit me again, I grabbed the folding chair I had been sitting in and held it up to protect myself. The next time he wound up to hit me, I struck first and smacked him in the ankles with the chair, dropping him to the ground. I quickly snatched his music stand as he fell and rammed the flat part under his chin.

"You remember me as a stooge. That guy in class who always got picked on and always had the bad luck and always wound up in trouble."

"I remember a fucking—"

I pushed the edge of the music stand deeper into his neck. "Whatever you remember of me is gone," I said. "The stooge is dead and what you're messing with now is something new. Something I can't control. So stay the fuck away from me, understand?"

He tried to nod but couldn't because of the music stand on his neck. I dropped the stand and walked away. No tagline needed.

Billy wasn't behind the desk at the hotel when I returned, and I was happy about that. I went to the business center and tried my best to find a way to change my flight to leave sooner without paying an outrageous fee but had no luck at all with it. I remembered him saying something about the hotel having pull with the airlines to get flights changed cheaper, but I suspected it was all baloney anyway just to get me away from him so he didn't catch my bad luck.

And to be honest, I didn't really want to go back. There was nothing good for me left in Detroit and this was a city I had always wanted to visit. It seemed like a great place to get lost, and without my phone and without my play to worry about, it seemed like the perfect time to just be absorbed into the city. I'd been a writer and a student and a husband and a father (sort of) and a patsy and now it was time for the next natural progression: tourist.

As I approached the Queensboro Plaza station for the

second time, my staring was minimal and I mostly kept to myself in my own thoughts. Before I could do any hardcore touristing, I needed to get to a bank, get a new debit card, and withdraw some cash. I wasn't terribly keen on wandering around the city with a wad of cash, but it would be the only option for the time being. And with the way I felt inside, I hoped the anger and the bitterness would be conveyed through my outward attitude and fend off any further street assaults.

I emerged from the 42nd Street station and was happily enveloped, once again, in its magic. There were a few different directions I could take and each played to a different part of who I was or who I thought I wanted to be. I could head up Broadway and wind my way through the side streets of the theater district and absorb every bit of theatrical magic I could find. If I was lucky, I could find cheap tickets to a non-musical play or, even better, a behind the scenes tour of a theater. Maybe I would even camp out in one of the diners famous in theater lore with a notebook and a pen and write my own play instead of relying on other people for my big break.

I could wander a few blocks away from the theater district into Hell's Kitchen where some of my favorite detective novels and comic books of the seventies had been set. Maybe I'd get the inspiration I needed to write the first in what would be my breakout and long-running detective series. Or maybe I'd stumble across one of those film crews people were always complaining about that snarled traffic and brought out the gawkers. Could it be my big break would be in film rather than books or theater? That actually was an exciting enough thought to start walking that way. I'd only taken a few steps though when a skinny teenager with an enormous personality handed me a flyer for a bus tour of the city.

Bam. The easy way to get to *all* the areas of the city I wanted to see. I told him I didn't have any cash and asked where the nearest branch of my bank was, and he pointed me down a few blocks more. The building itself looked like an abandoned restaurant on the outside, but inside it was a faded and slightly dated copy of the branch by my campus apartment in Detroit. I chatted with a delightful and incredibly tall woman about my account and what had happened to me and walked out a short time later with my wad of cash refilled, a provisional debit card in my pocket, and my faith in humanity temporarily restored.

I used ten bucks to buy an Iron Man wallet from a grizzled old Indian man on a decorative rug across from the bank. I put the rest of my cash, my new debit card, and the business card from the tour bus driver into the wallet and crammed it into my front pocket. I floated down the street, skipping a few steps every once in a while, and everything was going my way until I passed a Verizon store. It was another unassuming building stuck between a Subway and a Duane Reade, and I stood on the sidewalk staring inside the store, wondering if I should replace my phone and put an end to *that* adventure. The process would be easy and inexpensive since I had been talked into the full protection plan by my aggressive sales person when I bought the phone.

But I couldn't do it. I thought about however many emails I had waiting for me with location notes from my phone taunting me with how close the thief was and what a jackass I was. I didn't want those emails to stop. If I bought a new phone it would brick the old one and be like it never existed. A fresh start. But I didn't want a fresh start. I wanted revenge. If I was ever going to move forward in my life, that was the fresh start I needed. Proving to Dutchy and to myself that I wasn't a doormat for society anymore.

I bowed to the store window for no particular reason and cut over a few blocks and up back toward Times Square until I found the massive New York Public Library building on Bryant Park and asked the security guard where I could get internet access without a library card. She directed me to the third floor where a woman who looked to be about my age and shattered every stereotype I had ever encountered about librarians took pity on me and my lack of photo ID and granted me thirty minutes of guest access with a smile.

The first thing I did was plug the name of Dutchy's theater into Google to see what came up. The first page of results was split between d-level blog stories about his attempt to revive his career with the occasional wire brief that popped up on People.com or TMZ.com and stories about his recent arrest for fighting in an Orlando bar. But as I clicked through to the second and third pages of results, a more sinister story started to come together. When my thirty minutes of guest access was done, no one came to kick me off, but the computer shut down and asked me to log in again. I suppose I could have weaseled another thirty minutes out if I tried, but I had what I needed. I didn't like what I had, but that was a different story.

On the way out of the library, I thought about my late wife for the first time in months. I thought about her and the genuine love we briefly shared, and the fun times we had before I gunned her down in an abandoned dinosaur theme park where she tried to kill me. But for a brief moment in time, we had date night every Wednesday when the local library would get new release DVDs in. We had perfected a system to get them right when they came in and before things went sour, we'd been in the middle of binge watching *Breaking Bad*.

I desperately wished I was walking out of that library with the next disc of *Breaking Bad* rather than a plan to take on one of Queens's most notorious and dangerous drug dealers.

I had a plan but I needed a car. Even in New York City, I was sure there had to be a way to do surveillance without a car, but I didn't know what it was or how to find out. So I needed a car. Stealing one was out of the question because I had no idea how to hot wire anything and figured if I did manage to get away with it, I'd immediately get stuck in traffic, tied up perfectly while the police came to find me. Going back to Bizzy and Billy was out of the question too, and even if they would have worked with me, this was something I needed to do on my own. My credit was too bad to rent a car, and I'd lost one car and had another shot up with assault rifles the last time I used ZipCar, all of which left me with a handful of rotten options. There was one rotten option though that did have a few benefits though.

If the plan I hastily threw together in the library was going to have any chance of success, I needed people to continue underestimating me. Including Dutchy. While it felt good to let loose on him and show him my darker side, that didn't help me in the long run. So I spent a little time on the tour bus drinking from a bottle of discount whiskey I'd bought until I was sufficiently drunk and depressed to approach Dutchy again.

I wobbled up to the stage door again and prepared to knock, not quite sure what kind of reception I would get, but before I could bang on the door it opened up and Cristal Hate (real name Lenny Haight—yes legally Lenny, not Len or Leonard) the drug dealer I was hoping to spy on, walked out. I looked at his hulking frame—he had to be way over six feet tall and damn near close to six feet wide—and willed myself to keep quiet and get out of his way. But my brain had no pull with the rest of my body, so we all just stayed in the big man's path until he knocked me over.

"Shit," he said, with a surprising amount of concern. Then: "Hey, I know you?"

My brain was trying every trick it had to get an emergency message through to the rest of my body that shutting up was the only course of action with no success. So really, no matter how angry and bitter I believed I had become, I was not at all surprised when the goofy moron at my core looked up and said, "You're the drug dealer who owns this place."

Chapter Four

I expected to be thrown in the trunk of a car and taken to the long-term parking lot at JFK, but the big man looming over me held out a giant meaty hand and pulled me up from the street.

"You're Dutchy's guy," he said.

I was more drunk than I wanted to be and that led me to being more honest than I wanted to be.

"I am *not* Dutchy's anything," I said. "Maybe Dutchy's doom."

He grunted and stepped away from me.

"Should we talk or something," he said.

"I came to spy on you."

I could feel all the progress I'd made evaporating into the air along with the alcohol in my system. My moment as angry and aggressive Dominick was passing and all I was going to be left with was—

No. There was still some of that in me. I needed to fight for it. Push it.

"I have a car around the corner," he said. "Got some decent booze in the back and AC. This fucking humidity is going to—"

"Sure, let's go," I said.

I didn't vomit. Not on the way to the car and not in the car. He offered me a gin and tonic, which I declined, and then a giant bottle of water, which I sucked down like a desert survivor. We ended up back at the same bar I'd had my tough talk with Dutchy, but this time we bypassed the cramped bar area and headed upstairs to a palatial office suite out of something from MTV. I knew it was cool because I didn't get any of the décor or understand any of the awards. Best I could piece together was this notorious drug dealer had been putting together a series of legitimate business ventures in entertainment and sports.

"Have a seat," he said, pointing to a pair of uncomfortable-looking chairs in front of an enormous desk that looked like it had been designed by a car customizing shop: lots of chrome and bright colors and leather trim and accessories.

I worked my way into one of the chairs and he sat behind the desk and stared at me. He was probably trying to break me with awkward silence, but I wasn't going to break. I had a bunch of questions, but absolutely no way to frame them that didn't make me look worse than I already did.

We stared at each other for a long time and three people came into his office and whispered things in his ear before he finally broke the silence.

"I don't see it," he said.

"You and me both. But what can you do, right?"

He nodded and twisted in his chair. I wondered if I should try to leave.

"The thing is," he said, still twisting in the chair, "is I'm not really taking on any more writers."

Uh…

"Pardon?"

"I know Dutchy set you up with this big premier and all and he thinks it's going to be some sort of showcase that will make people forget he's been an asshole most of his adult life, but I just don't get it."

"Okay."

"Don't say much, do you? Dutchy pitched you as some sort of big chatter head. Won't shut up."

"Dutchy doesn't know me anymore."

He nodded again and took something out of his front shirt pocket. It was a glossy business card with his name and an email address on it with a small and elaborate logo in the bottom corner.

"Nice name," I said.

"Probably woulda picked something less stupid these days, but it's still better than the name my momma gave me. Anyway, sports and music are my things," he said. "A bit of movie stuff, but that shit baffles me to no end. I like you though."

"Okay," I said, amazing myself with my restraint.

"When this thing with Dutchy is over, come talk to me, we'll see what we can make happen."

I really didn't want to say okay again and nodding seemed like co-opting his move, so I stood up and held out my hand. He shook it and nodded. Twenty minutes later I was back outside Dutchy's theater, wondering if the entire thing had been a dream.

Dutchy's screeching voice and suspiciously timed appearance disavowed me of that notion.

"The hell were you doing with him? You goin' behind my back? You—"

"Just. Shut. Up," I said, holding up my hand. "You were right."

"Of course I was. 'Bout time you came to realize it."

"You're still a jackass, but that doesn't mean—"

"Goddammit I'm not gonna stand here and have you bad mouth me in front of my own—"

"Seriously, if this is going to work between us, you've got to learn to keep your mouth shut sometimes."

Even as the words were rolling out of my mouth, I realized how cocky and arrogant I sounded and how wrong that was for the mood I needed to be cultivating. I needed to take my own damn advice and learn when the hell to keep my mouth shut. Dutchy's face was an unhealthy shade of red and the veins along his cheeks and forehead were throbbing. I needed to shut him down quickly, so I used the only quick acting tool I had in my pocket: casual racism.

I'd tried so hard over the last couple of years to move beyond the entitled white academic cocoon I lived in and I gave up every last bit of the miniscule progress I'd made when I said, "I'm sorry man, I don't know what came over me. Just being with guys like him, with *those* people, freaks me out."

"*Those* people?"

"You know," I said. "His kind of people. Their culture?"

"Jesus, Dominick. This is the twenty-first century. You can't be saying shit like that."

I immediately freaked out and wondered how I had suddenly become less progressive and aware than a guy who had worn a sexy Hitler costume to a campus Halloween party. But then he bobbed his head up and down taking in our surroundings and pushed me into the theater.

"What the—"

"Say shit like that out in the street and you'll get us both gunned down, Jesus."

Okay, so I was still awful, but at least I was better than Dutchy for the time being.

"Right, right," I said. "Still getting used to this city."

"Not sure how you survived Detroit, but I guess that doesn't matter. You're back. So tell me what you talked about with our friend Mr. Haight."

"I didn't find out anything," I said, squashing the urge to let him know I knew Hate's real name. "I think he wants to sign me to his label or agency or whatever it is he has."

"The hell a guy like that want with a dopey little cracker like you?"

"No clue, but he gave me his card and said when I was done working with you to maybe give him a call and see what we could work on together."

"That all sounds like bullshit. I bet he was feeling you out, seeing what you know."

"I don't know anything."

"And for once," Dutchy said. "That's going to be an asset."

I tried hard not to roll my eyes as he laid out his plan for me. It was light on specifics and heavy on bullshit, but the basics lined up with what I'd learned at the library. In addition to being a noted drug dealer cum entertainment agent, Lenny Haight was one of Queens worst slum lords. He'd been investigated and charged dozens of times but nothing major ever stuck. It was an endless parade of dropped charges when witness failed to appear and settlements for peanuts when his lawyers did manage to get hold of a witness. Nobody ever really cared though because most of his properties were in poor neighborhoods and rented out to poor people. The one exception was the Tate Theater, a former strip club in a former industrial wasteland that had, in recent years, suddenly become trendy.

Ownership changed hands through a couple of shady shell corporations that could circumstantially be traced back to Haight, but what really stood out, and what I suspected I'd been lured to town for, was a three-million-dollar fraudulent mortgage that had been taken out, in cash, on the theater, and then absconded with. The cops had looked into it until the investigating officer was blown up in his car and the treasury department had looked into it until one of their agents was killed in a mugging gone bad in the alley behind the theater. Private citizens looking into the money for less community-oriented reasons hadn't fared any better. The list of dead bodies associated with that one single theater was nine.

"And you want me to be number ten," I said.

"No way, that would be shitty for both of us. But you're invincible to this shit, man. You're the perfect guy for this."

I wanted to smack him, maybe even punch him again and curse at him and go crazy, but pushed that all down and repressed it for the bigger goal. There was only so much repression I was capable of, so I needed to make the most of what I could muster.

"I thought you'd at least try to deny it for a bit before admitting you brought me here as bait," I said.

"Dom, buddy, come on," he said, putting his arm around me. "Bait is such a rotten word. I want you to be my partner."

"Huh," I said. "Okay. Where do we start?"

"That's all you, man. That's your gig. Your *thing*.

Just go be you and wait for the trouble to find you."

"Huh," I said again. "Okay."

I was getting twitchy again and needed to get away from Dutchy before I did something I couldn't take back, so I gave him a thumbs up and left the theater and went back to my hotel. I had no idea what time it was, but the city was dark, and I'd been up since four a.m. to make my flight, and the recharge from my little nap at the hotel earlier had long worn off. I needed to get somewhere with a bed, get a few drinks in me to take the edge off, and see if I could think better in the morning when I didn't want to murder everyone who came near me.

There was a stocky Latina of indeterminate age with a name tag that said her name was Kelly behind the counter when I finally calmed myself down enough to present myself as a reasonable facsimile of a proper human being. My room key had been lost some time during this longest day ever, so I was going to need to ask for a new one, bringing with it so many opportunities for shit to find me.

Dutchy had been right about that being my *thing*, and I had complete faith that my bad luck would eventually lead me to the money we were looking for—the question was if I could survive my luck before finding it and after. Since Billy had already worked a shift earlier in the day, I hoped he hadn't been back since our car ride after his shift to make any notes on my account that would affect my stay.

"I, uh…I lost my room key," I said, trying too hard to sound normal. "Can I get a new one?"

She nodded and typed in the information I gave her to verify my reservation. I found myself actually crossing my fingers while she waited for verification. All I needed was some sleep, maybe a shower, maybe a comforting movie on HBO. What I got was:

"There seems to be a problem with your reservation."

Chapter Five

"No," I said. "There's no problem. I had a key earlier. I actually slept in that room, took a shower in that room, all of the things I want to do...*need* to do right now. So no problem. Just a new key. Because I'm scatterbrained. That's all. NO FUCKING PROBLEM."

I probably shouldn't have said that last thing.

It reminded me of this time I was with my former wife at a Golden Corral buffet.

She was pregnant and all she wanted was some cotton candy and the lazy people behind the counter were laughing at us and telling us the machine was broken even though we could see it was working. So I found a fat little pig of a manager in tight, white short sleeves and a stained black tie, and told him our problem. He insisted the machine was broken even as I pointed to show him the clerks were using it for themselves right at that minute. He finally agreed to go over and talk to them while I stood and watched. When he was done, I went over again and asked for cotton candy; they again told me the machine was broken; I again went and told this all to the manager. He stuck to his guns, said I was the one

at fault, so I called him a number of names and threw an
f-bomb in there, and he threw us out. I screamed the
entire way out and, frankly, was surprised the cops
hadn't been called.

But that was a different me. A less angry me. A less
violent me.

To her credit, Kelly remained very calm as she told
me to wait in the lobby for the police to arrive even as
she had to call hotel security to hold me because I was
less than cooperative. Two guys who looked more like
management interns than security goons forced me
down into a chair, and I really think the beefier of the
two was ready to sit on me if I hadn't given up out of
sheer exhaustion. By the time an unmarked police cruiser
pulled up to the hotel, I was asleep.

A plainclothes cop in jeans and a Hilton Head, South
Carolina tourism shirt with an NYPD shield hanging
from his neck shook me awake and escorted me to his
car. As I got in the back, my brain shot awake with all
the possibilities of where we could be going. My first
thought was that Bianca the Uber driver had been found
murdered and they had linked her to me through my
stuff but then I also wondered if he was a crooked cop
who was also looking for the missing money and was
going to torture me to find out what I knew. The truth was
far less exciting and not at all what I needed right then.

On the way to wherever we were going, he explained
that his name was Paul Guyot and the shield around his
neck was from the Secret Service, not the NYPD.

"Holy shit," I said, briefly excited again. "Is Dutchy
trying to kill the president?"

"The hotel flagged your account as part of an operation they're working with us on to cut down on the

amount of counterfeit currency running through—"

"No," I said. "This is a mistake. I haven't used any cash, counterfeit or otherwise."

He ignored my pleas the entire rest of the drive. I kept expecting us to cross one of the bridges and head into Manhattan, but we never did and the further we got out of Queens, the more worried I became that in fact this was a crooked cop with a really boring cover story. But eventually we pulled into a bland parking structure in a bland area of slightly taller buildings that kind of looked like a mini downtown area.

"Welcome to Brooklyn," he said.

And then he got out of the car and left me in it. I waited for him to return but he never did. It was daybreak before I realized I'd been had. I tried to unlock the doors but they wouldn't budge. There was no radio in the car, which surprised me from what I knew about police cruisers, even unmarked ones, and nothing else about the car gave any clues to a potential escape.

So I kicked the windows. I laid on my back like I'd seen on a hundred different *Dateline* specials and put my whole effort into planting both of my feet squarely at the center of the window and stomping. But nothing happened. Then I remembered police cruisers have bullet-proof windows specifically to prevent such an escape and I became so enraged I stomped even harder and faster. And damned if the window didn't explode into a hundred fractured lines and then pop out.

I wiggled out of the car and ran down the stairs of the parking structure to the street. I was standing in front of a Marriott hotel and to my right was a building so generic looking it had to be a government office tower. I was heading toward the entrance when I saw my friend

41

the Secret Service agent exiting. He'd traded the jeans and T-shirt for black dress pants and a white dress shirt but I recognized him anyway.

"You," I yelled. "What the hell?"

He must not have been expecting anyone to yell at him, so he kept walking toward the parking garage. Instead of yelling again, I followed him into the garage. I remained quiet until we reached his car and he saw the broken window.

"Awww, dammit," he muttered.

"How do you think I feel?"

He turned toward me this time, but I didn't get the satisfaction of recognition I'd hoped for.

"Just be cool, man," he said. "You can have the car and I'll even get you my wallet. I just need to—"

"You locked me in your car last night and left me there."

"Oh, shit. Why did you break my window?"

"You *locked* me in your fucking car."

"And you couldn't unlock the door? Are you so hopped up on whatever that—"

"I tried. But it's got cop locks, duh. Don't pin this on me."

He ran to the car and opened the back door with the broken window.

"This is my personal vehicle," he said. "No cop locks."

"Do it from the inside. I'm not a moron."

He closed the back door and went around to the driver's side door and opened it.

"I don't have time for this. Just get out of here and stay out of trouble."

I ran to the car this time and banged on his window

until he rolled it down.

"I didn't use any counterfeit bills at that hotel. I used a debit card."

"Must have been a mistake then. My bad. Have a nice—"

I reached my hand inside his window and grabbed for his throat.

"I'm having a really bad couple of days," I screamed. "And this is *not* helping."

He'd obviously had enough of my nonsense, which I suppose I should have seen coming, because instead of just driving away, he swung his door open into my body with a snap that flung me backward onto the pavement with a grunt. By the time I regained my breath and the feeling in my ass, Guyot was standing over me with a handgun pointed at my chest.

"My last few days haven't been a fucking vacation either. I hate this city and all I want to do is drink my pop to get the caffeine flowing so I can stay awake long enough to get—"

"Did you say pop?"

I scooted away from him and sat up; he tightened his grip on the gun and pushed it toward me.

"I did what I was supposed to and got you out of Queens and thought you'd be smart enough to—"

"You're from Michigan, aren't you?"

He dropped his gun to his side and stepped back toward his car. "I'm giving you one more chance to get out of here before I have to…"

"Have to what? Who sent you? Was it my wife's family?"

"Just go, kid. Come on."

I rushed him and slammed him into his car which

knocked his gun out of his hand and a few feet away. We both rushed for it, but I got it and held it away from him.

"Tell me who sent you."

"I tried to make it right, the gambling. It's just...man..."

"Were you supposed to kill me?"

He looked at me for a few seconds without saying anything then nodded.

"But you let me go?"

"Word is you're going to get yourself killed one of these days anyway so I just hoped...I couldn't do it."

"Corrupt cop with a heart of gold?"

"Fuck you."

I handed him his gun back but didn't walk away.

"Probably wouldn't be the worst thing if somebody took me out," I said. "End of my rope's got to be pretty close."

"They're *everywhere*, you know."

"And they blame me for everything?"

"They blame plenty of other people too, but yeah, you're a popular target."

I nodded. "Thought this city was big enough to hide for a while."

"Just keep your head up and don't trust anyone."

"Not even you?"

"Just go."

I went and when I exited on to the street, I thought I heard a gunshot but tried not to think too much about what that meant. It was obvious my time in the city needed to come to an end soon, but wherever I was going to go next, I needed to go with a plan and enough money to hide and stay hidden. To do that, I needed to find Dutchy's money and get it out of town before he or Cristal Hate found out. Before I could even attempt to think of a plan that could come close to having a chance at success, I needed to sleep. The Marriott I was standing in front of seemed like a good enough place to start.

Chapter Six

I had no trouble getting a room at the Marriot and had no trouble falling asleep once I hit the bed. It was such an easy time, in fact, I briefly forgot where I was and what I was up to. I had a dream about flying hot dogs in space that transitioned into a weird kind of Wizard of Oz dream, and when I woke up, enough of the details lingered in my head that I sat down at the desk, with the *Today Show* on in the background, and wrote the opening for a satirical science fiction story that I had no idea what to do with. But it felt good to write. It felt even better to be using my imagination instead of just transcribing lightly fictionalized versions of the trouble in my own life. I wrote for an hour and in that brief but wonderful bubble, I was in control. I was useful. I was good.

Real life intruded through a call from the front desk. I didn't ask who it was, just told them I'd meet the person downstairs in five. And I spent four of those five minutes sitting at the desk, twirling the pen in my fingers, contemplating what kind of man I wanted to be. I was never going to be a good man. I didn't have the drive or the constitution for good works. I did think, though, that there was a path forward as a sacrificial sort of bad guy—a sin eater of sorts—where maybe if I did enough of the right bad things that helped enough actual good people, I might at least lessen my eternal damnation and maybe aim for some sort of heavenly wildcard. And if the afterlife turned out to be the great lie I hoped it was, then I could at least spend the rest of my life alleviating my guilt rather than wallowing in it.

I jotted down a few more lines in the story and went back up to the top of the page and added a title and my byline. I was too vain to ever use a pen name, and that, ultimately, would be my downfall in life. Whether I scored enough money from Dutchy to disappear or not would be a moot point if I kept publishing stuff under my own name that made me easy to find. So I needed to find a way to keep my wife's family from hunting me down and murdering me out of revenge for her death that still allowed me the freedom to publish under my real name. I wasn't quite sure what that would turn out to be, but I didn't suspect it was going to be anything to be proud of.

When I walked into the lobby of the hotel to meet my mystery visitor, I didn't know what to expect. But I was pretty sure there was one person I could expect not to see: Bianca, the thieving Uber driver. I wanted to immediately go to her and grab her and pin her down until she told me why she robbed me, but she was talking to the concierge and I couldn't help but eavesdrop.

"He said he'd leave the tickets here," she said. "And my dad never lies. He's a Secret Service agent for god's sake. I don't think they're allowed to…"

I didn't hear anything else she said, or the concierge's response, because I was trying to convince myself this

47

was a big fucking coincidence and not the life-altering tear in the fabric of my existence that it really was.

I took three deliberate steps toward her, hoping to hear something that would neutralize my dread, but all I heard was a shrieking voice behind me say, "If you think Queens is a shithole, Brooklyn is going to rot your fucking mind, dude."

I turned to see Dutchy with his arms wide open, then I snapped back to see if Bianca had turned around as well. She was still going at it with the concierge, so I ran to Dutchy.

"Tell me you hired her," I said, pointing to Bianca. "I can deal with anything you tell me, as long as you tell me the truth."

"I paid for your hotel, why the hell would I hire somebody to—"

"I'm paying for my own hotel, goddammit. You were supposed to hire me a car. And please tell me that girl was the one you hired."

He threw his arms in the air and rolled his eyes.

"Don't know what your fucking drug is, dude, but I've never seen that broad in my life."

"Fuck," I said. "Fuck fuck fuck."

Dutchy smiled and opened his mouth to say something, but I cut him off with my hand.

"Don't you dare."

He shrugged. "Whatever. We need to talk."

"Gimme a few minutes. I need to talk to that girl."

Dutchy smiled wide and nodded. "Oh yeah, I got it good, buddy. Need a wing man?"

It wasn't worth the time or effort trying to explain to him what was actually going on, so I put my arm around his shoulder and whispered in his ear.

"I can't imagine a better wing man than you," I said. "But I'm still new with this girl and she's kind of shy and in a bubble, you know?"

"I got it, I got it. I might be too much man for her."

Too much something, I thought. But I choked out a smile and nodded.

"Just need a minute and then we can talk."

Dutchy faded back into the crowd by the entrance and I approached Bianca. She was deep in conversation with a tall man in a dark suit, who I assumed was a manager, so I put my hand on her arm and cleared my throat.

"I think I can help," I said.

They both turned to look at me and I was a bit surprised that she didn't recognize me. But it really shouldn't have. She might have been the focus of every single one of my waking thoughts, but I was probably just one of many stupid marks she encountered in a given day.

"We're in the middle of something," she snapped.

"Hence the offer to help. I know where your tickets are."

She turned away from me to look back at the manager.

"Is this a joke? We've had problems with this desk before and I told my dad not to leave the tickets here but—"

"It's not a joke," I said. "I talked to your dad this morning."

She looked at me and then back to the manager, who looked confused and desperate to be done with the conversation.

"My dad is a man of intense habit," she said. "Not the sort who involves random strangers in his plans."

"Maybe we should step off to the side," I said. "And let this gentleman get back to work so he doesn't call

49

security on us."

They both continued staring at me awkwardly, but finally Bianca relented and stepped off to the side with me. I looked around to see if Dutchy was still nearby, but I didn't see him.

"Listen," Bianca said. "I know what I did was shitty but—"

"Was it your dad who asked you to pick me up and dump me?"

She didn't say anything, but her body language hinted I was on the right track.

"I'm not here for revenge or anything," I said. "You're just a piece of something bigger."

"How philosophical."

"Petty and vindictive is more like it."

I explained to her that I really had spoken with her dad that morning and let her in on most of what happened without mentioning the final shot I heard after I left him. None of it seemed to shock her.

"I thought he followed me out here because he didn't think I'd be safe," she said. "But the last week or so he's been a mess."

"They were squeezing him pretty hard I'm guessing."

"So this is your fault?"

I shrugged. "Not entirely," I said. "But I haven't exactly helped the situation."

"Fine. We're even, or whatever. But I really do need those tickets. Did my dad give you any indication where he might have left them?"

"Shit," I said.

"No..."

"I can't say anything for sure. But...Well, let me show you."

I led her up to the top of the parking garage where I'd left her dad and paused before exiting the stairwell.

"He was pretty freaked out when I left him," I said. "And…I just…I don't know what's out there, but I want you do be prepared for the worst."

She was. I wasn't. Because the worst-case scenario wasn't seeing a body on the ground, it was seeing the car still there with a blood spot where I'd left him but no body. Somebody picked him up or cleaned him up. Either way, that was bad news for me. Maybe for both of us.

While I circled the car looking for any sign of something less nefarious, Bianca went through the car looking for her tickets. She found them in the glovebox and waved them at me.

"We're good," she said. "I gotta go."

"No way. We're in this together. And you still have my stuff."

"I really can't. I promise we'll hook up later and I'll get you your stuff."

She was into the stairwell and on the street before I could catch up. The same car she picked me up in was illegally parked in front of the hotel and all I could do was watch from the street as she drove away.

I went back in to look for Dutchy who was nowhere to be found so I headed back up to the top of the parking garage and sat in the car wondering what in the hell to do next.

Chapter Seven

Dutchy found me twenty minutes later still sitting in the death car. Sure I was creeped out that he always seemed to know where I was at any given time, but that was part of the luck or karma or whatever it was that made me a trouble magnet that I was hoping to finally use in my favor. So when he showed up, I didn't think about the whys or hows, just looking for what move I could make to push my game forward. In this case, he provided a ride, at minimum.

"I thought I was escaping," I told him, in a rare moment of emotional honesty.

"I got guys," he said. "Get a couple of goons on you and it won't matter what they throw at you."

"There aren't enough goons in the world to stop them if they really want to get to me. And there's no telling how many innocent people I'm putting in harm's way in the meantime."

"Ain't no innocent people 'round these parts," he said, dropping into a rural sound I'd always known him to have even though he'd never really spent any significant time in a rural environment. "Case that makes you feel better."

"What would make me feel better would be showing up back in Detroit and gunning down every single one of the motherfuckers gunning for me."

"Bam," Dutchy said. "Let's do it. I got the goons and the guns. You've got the brains and the GPS for trouble."

I'd been thinking the same thing. But it was a line I wasn't willing to cross. I could see myself approaching a defining moment in my life and my legacy and I had to be very careful not to snap. There was no more denying my violent nature, but I didn't want to get twitchy about it. When I snapped I wanted it to mean something. I also wanted to make sure I had the gravitas of experience to pull it off when the time came as well. I didn't want to have to kill any more people than was necessary just because I couldn't project any confidence in my mission.

"We've still got work here to do," I said. "That money will make a huge difference in the options I have available to me."

"And capping a few big city assholes along the way can't be bad for your rep either."

I nodded absentmindedly, wondering how much to leave to chance and how much to work through and plan out. I'd always been a stream of consciousness writer and that style of living had worked well enough for me to that point in life as well. But there were so many elements, so many chances for something to slip through and screw it all up, that I was tempted to try and subvert the obvious problem at least.

But Dutchy kept pushing me so I would keep lurching forward and let the chips—and the bodies—fall where they may.

"You've got a car here, right?"

"Do I look like the public transportation sort?"

"Let's get back to the theater then. And while you drive, you can tell me everything you know about Bianca and how big of a pain in our asses you think she might be."

"We'd have to drive damn near to Maine for me to tell you everything about that goofy broad."

"Goofy though, that's good, right? Goofy can't be dangerous."

"Sure, she's goofy as hell and cute to boot. But she's a flake and she's given mixed messages to a pile of all the wrong kinds of dudes."

"Like Cristal Hate?"

"Like Cristal Hate ain't even the nastiest dude she's burned and strung along."

"Huh," I said. "I feel like I'm in good company."

Dutchy also had a car illegally parked in front of the hotel and I was a bit struck by how much that illegal action bothered me and how frustrating and unfair it seemed compared to other shadier stuff I'd been part of. I felt even worse when I got into the back seat with him and saw Big Bizzy behind the wheel and Billy from the hotel desk in the passenger's seat.

"Jesus Christ," I said, looking at Dutchy. "Is there anything you haven't lied to me about?"

"Lied sounds so nasty, man. I was feeling you out. Testing you, you know?"

"Bullshit."

"It's not like you made yourself easy to understand either, man. First few times we met it was nothing but rambling nonsense coming out of you. Had to get you settled down before I could see what you really were."

"And what am I? Really?"

"A badass motherfucker."

He held up a fist to be bumped and I obliged, though I doubted the title. I suspected I wasn't the only one in the car who felt that way either. I spent the rest of the drive back to Queens explaining what had happened and quizzing them on what else was really going on. I was uncharacteristically honest and hoped that would make for more useful information.

"Bianca Dade," Bizzy said, after a while. "We warned you about her."

"At the time, I took your advice. But now, her ex-boyfriend or husband or life partner or whatever she was with Cristal Hate is not the most dangerous person she's associated with."

"It's you," Bizzy said.

"Not quite, but yeah. My family. My wife's family. Ex-wife."

"You divorced a mobbed-up woman?"

"My boy didn't divorce her," Dutchy said. "He blew the bitch away."

I turned to Dutchy and smacked him.

"Watch your fucking mouth," I said.

Dutchy reached over at my neck but I swatted his hands away. Bizzy slammed on the brakes and sent both of us slamming into the seats in front of us. When I shook off the daze, I saw Billy pointing a gun at us.

"Calm down or we'll dump you both in The Hole."

I looked at Dutchy for some idea of what they meant but he gave me a blank stare and a shrug. The last vestiges of common sense that operated on the fringes of my consciousness pushed back any thought I had of asking more about it, but the writer part of me that was more dormant than absent, lit up and took over the show.

"The Hole some kind of dungeon?" I asked.

Billy looked over at Bizzy, who was putting the car back in gear, and smiled at him.

"Our boy here has some questions about The Hole," he said.

Bizzy nodded. I couldn't see if he was smiling or not.

"Actually makes some sense," Bizzy said. "Got a cousin in Howard Beach might be able to set us up for a bit while we sort this all out."

"Nobody gonna come looking for us in The Hole," Billy said.

"No. Not a single person gonna come out to look for us in The Hole."

I immediately regretted asking about The Hole.

"Welcome to New York City's own seedy border town," Billy said. "The neighborhood that time, and gentrification, forgot."

I'd tried track our journey to figure out where we were headed, and as best as I could tell, we were on the border between Queens and Brooklyn out near JFK airport, though from the views out my window, we were in the slums of a third world country. The buildings were dilapidated and leaning away from the street and from each other. Many of the bigger buildings still had a bit of their concrete lower levels, but the top levels were all stripped iron. And every patch of grass and most of the street was overgrown with weeds. I'd seen areas in worse parts of Detroit that seemed like luxury resorts in comparison.

"You want the wild west," Bizzy said, "They got actual cowboys out here. The Federation of Black Cowboys. Stick around more than a few minutes and you'll see 'em riding around keeping the peace and shooting the rats."

We pulled off of the main road and drove through a puddle roughly the size of Lake Michigan and emerged in a wooded lot near what looked like an abandoned Winnebago RV. Bizzy pulled the car right up next to the RV and turned the car off. When we got out of the car, we were rushed inside the RV, which turned out not to be abandoned at all but rather cleverly disguised, while Bizzy grabbed a massive black tarp from a barrel next to the RV and draped it over the car. I'd been in any number of situations where I was certain I was standing in my final resting place, but none had me quite so certain as I was standing on the steps of that RV watching a man I didn't trust hide the car he drove me in.

Bizzy pushed me inside and I saw that in addition to everyone who had arrived in our car, there were three other people in the RV who looked a lot like Bizzy.

"That's Old Harold," Bizzy said, pointing to a man who looked like a computer-aged version of Bizzy in thirty years. "My cousin's cousin or some shit like that. And that scrawny pissant over by the steering wheel is Baby Harold, no relation, and that fine, fine lady over in the back by the chemical toilet is my auntie Seal. Everyone say hello."

We murmured our hellos and milled about looking for extra space to accommodate all of us. I wondered if they would shoot us one at a time out back or shoot us both at the same time right here and then burn the RV. Instead they offered us booze from the chemical toilet. Something called an Ejector Seat that tasted like a mix of cheap bourbon and mint tea. It wasn't half bad and did an admirable job of dulling the pain and jitters of the last few days. By the time I finished, I couldn't have cared less where they would take me to kill me.

But they didn't kill me. They helped me. Sort of. Bizzy and Billy left with Old Harold and Baby Harold, no relation, leaving Dutchy and I alone with Auntie Seal.

"Given name is Cecelia," she said, heading to the toilet for another round of drinks. "You know, like that Simon and Garfunkel song."

"My parents loved that song," Dutchy said.

"Course they did," she said. "White people love that stuff. So did my parents. Kids in the neighborhood though, not so much. Started calling me Seal in grade school and it just stuck. Now I can't imagine living without it."

"I apologize," I said. "And maybe it's the booze talking, but why are we here with you exactly?"

"Well if you don't know, son, then I don't see how I can help you."

"Uh, I think, Ms. Seal, you can help us with some information, some background maybe, if you don't mind, about an old friend of yours."

"Oh shit," I said, sensing where he was going with his comment. "Did you date Cristal Hate?"

She made a humming noise and took a long swig of her drink then nodded.

"Long time ago. Not sure what I can tell you about what he's become."

"I, uh," this was Dutchy again, "I think we don't care so much about the person but his business, the older business…before the music and stuff."

Same humming noise, but this time she smiled.

"Ahhhhhhh, I see now," she said. "You boys seeing dollar signs."

"I think at this point at least," I said, "We're more in an information gathering mode."

"And you want me to tell you secrets about how to find the money everyone thinks he stole?"

"What do you mean thinks?" I asked. "Is there doubt?"

Dutchy ignored my line of questioning and continued harping on what he wanted.

"I brought my boy Dominick out here because he can find the money. I have no doubt about that—"

"Brought me out here on a lie, by the way."

"We're storytellers, man. I just gave you the narrative you needed to make it work for you."

"What did you mean about *thinking* he stole the money?"

"You boys need to probably look somewhere else for your beer money. This is out of your league."

"Goddammit, woman. This isn't what we need right now," Dutchy said. "I've been bringing my boy here along slowly and—"

"Just stop it," I said to Dutchy. Then I turned to Seal and tipped my cup outward for her to toast it, which she did. "He's right though, I'm a bit of a loose cannon. I don't think things through very well, if at all, and I live life almost entirely by the seat of my pants. I'm a danger to those around, but not to myself. Usually. And that's why we're here."

She took another swig of her drink and nodded slowly. "I heard of people like you, got what they call the curse of survival."

"That sounds about right," I said.

"Doesn't sound like much of a curse to me," Dutchy said.

"It's like being a vampire, but without the sex appeal. You're doomed to live a long, long life on this earth, but the cost of your survival is not blood, not directly at least, but you'll be the death of everyone you love."

"I'm already deep down that rabbit hole. But I'm looking to make the most of it. To see if I can...I don't know, use it for good sounds corny and I certainly want to make sure I profit from it, but I don't want to be an asshole about it anymore."

"This place they brought you, they call it The Hole. More Tri-State area assholes are buried in the fields and foundations and marshes out there than anywhere else. You've come to the right place."

"Can you help us?"

"You remind me of him," she said, pointing to me. "He's got a touch of the curse."

I felt like I'd been dropped into a weird street version of a voodoo pirate story, but I wasn't laughing. This woman had an intensity in her body language that spoke to massive life trauma, so I nodded like a bobble head and hoped to survive long enough to hear something useful. But I not only had to survive The Hole, and survive my own curse, I had to survive Dutchy's increasingly twitchy behavior. He'd never been one for asking for help or letting others take charge of his life, so this whole thing was just one giant stick of dynamite shoved up his ass waiting for an ignitor.

"This is *bullshit*," he said, throwing his cup to the floor and rushing Seal.

She easily dodged him and sent him flying into the small dining area, smacking his head on the table bolted to the floor. He popped up quickly after that, but he was woozy. His eyes were rolling around unnaturally in his head and he was wobbly on his feet. So I punched him. Once in the nose and once in the stomach. And then I wrapped my hands around his neck and held on for dear life as he shook and squirmed and spasmed.

He kneed me once in the groin, but I kept my grip around his neck until he finally began to fade. Seal watched from above, never making a move toward intervention.

"He was going to be in my way," I said.

She nodded and took two steps away from me.

Chapter Eight

"We have to wait until dark to dump him," Bizzy said. "So have fun starin' at your boy for the next few hours."

Bizzy, Billy, and the Harolds showed up at the RV just a few minutes after I'd done away with Dutchy, and I wondered if they'd known something was up and just gave me the space to do what I was meant to do all along. While I'd thought about killing Dutchy before, it had mostly been in the fantasy sort of way I imagined myself doing lots of different things I'd never expect to do in real life. But Dutchy's lifeless body was a pale, quickly ripening reminder of what I'd done. I wanted to be rid of it, but I circled back around to Seal's mention of the curse of survival.

"He wasn't my boy," I said to Bizzy, then I turned to Seal. "And he wasn't anyone I loved or cared about."

She nudged his body a bit out of the way and I cringed.

"Doesn't look like it to me," she said.

"I'm not evil," I said. "Not intentionally evil. This sort of stuff bothers me, no matter who it is. Isn't that good? Isn't that human?"

"Sounds like bullshit excuses to me," Bizzy said. "'Cause your boy still dead and we all still stuck in this little trailer until it gets dark enough to go dump him in a hole 'round the corner."

"We just dump him, and he goes away?"

"Maybe his body, but his spirit will always be in your heart," Bizzy said, holding his hand in the middle of his chest. "And probably in your house haunting you like a motherfucker."

I was feeling light-headed and needed to sit down. But there was no place to sit. The chemicals in my system, both natural and man-made, were wearing off and the full gravity of what I'd done was setting in.

"Anywhere but here," Seal said, sounding more clichéd and irritated than mystical. "That's where you want to be, isn't it?"

"I'm very claustrophobic and this place, and him, his…it's all just too much."

Billy was sitting in the driver's seat of the RV and had been quiet until right then.

"I could use a navigator," he said.

That sounded just fine, so I stepped toward him, but Bizzy cut me off, picked up Dutchy by the arms, and shoved him up into the passenger's seat. He crossed Dutchy's arms so he looked vaguely contemplative.

Auntie Seal was having none of it though. She clapped her hands together loud enough to echo in my ears long after she was done talking. I was only able to surmise what she said from reading her lips.

"That man is not a doll. We all have lived our lives to the glory of our bodies, and I will not have anyone treated that way in my presence."

Bizzy shifted on his feet awkwardly before finally

smacking Billy and working with him to get the body out of the front seat. Billy used his elbows to clear a path to the small dining table where Dutchy had met his demise and tried to sit him up in one of those seats like Dutchy was holding court in a bar. He would have probably loved that, but it still wasn't what Seal had in mind. She flung her arms out wide and knocked everyone back to the edges of the RV while she stomped to Dutchy's body. Using surprisingly robust upper body strength for a small woman, she flitted around the table and an adjoining counter until Dutchy was laid in state across the table with his arms folded respectfully over his chest.

"This is not a spiritual house," Seal said. "But we're a respectful house. So say something."

She was looking directly at me when she said that.

"Oh, I don't think that's wise for any—"

"You've made us implicit in your crime and you've soiled our home with your curse," she said. "Make an effort."

I had no desire to be a spiritual person. It was in my best interest for my life to be done and over when I took my last breath, not carried on in an afterlife. But I wondered if there was any sort of local network type of spirituality. Something I could use to gauge my life in terms of goals and good deeds and bad deeds with a bit of nuance. You know, where most people have their conscience.

I bounced back and forth on the tips of my toes and opened and closed my fists a few times. The first time I tried to speak I had to choke back tears. Any number of weeks ago I would have thrown up. It would have been a glorious purge that, through the detox of waste exiting my body and the humility of embarrassment, would have been all I needed as far as cleansing and forgiveness. But I was beyond purging anymore. It was all going to stick to me from then on out. So I just had to deal with it. And the only way I still knew how to deal with things was to tell a story.

"Dutchy was an asshole who brought me out here to trick me," I said by way of eulogy. "And I killed him for it, which he didn't deserve. He didn't deserve much of the shit life hung on him. He wasn't blessed like me."

I looked over at Seal to see if I was headed in the right direction. She shrugged and looked away. Bizzy and Billy were whispering to each other and Old Harold had fallen asleep standing up.

"I have to look at him like this forever," I continued. "Even when he's not here, like this, he'll rot my brain with the others. The others. Jesus, I never thought there'd be any, let alone *others*. And I'm sure there will be more. I won't go to jail. I'll be lucky if I'm murdered quickly by someone I think I trust, but more likely I'll just keep living. And when the curse is finally broken, when I'm finally allowed to die, I'll find Dutchy in hell and he'll still remember me. He'll smile at me and offer me whatever shit for booze they have down there and give me tips for making the best of it. So fuck me and my curse, and fuck you all. I hope this RV doesn't explode when I leave."

Nobody followed me when I left. They were probably happy to be rid of me. I clenched my fists and released them several more times as I walked back toward a subway station we'd past driving in. I was enraged and overly righteous. I hoped someone tried to mug me. I hoped *a group* tried to mug me. Instead I found a cluster of beat cops on a corner who asked me what in the hell I was doing out by myself.

"Murdered a guy in a trailer," I said, "and left before they buried him because they have to wait until dark so nobody sees them and there's no fucking way I'm staying in that little fucking RV with a guy I just killed so I don't get caught."

I wanted them to hit me. I wanted them to kick me or shoot me or drown me in one of the massive puddles everywhere. What I didn't count on them doing was ignoring me.

There were no cabs around so I walked. And walked. And walked some more. I walked enough that I wondered if I was the main character in an epic quest novel. But I needed the walk. I had excess energy and rage to burn and enough thinking to do to occupy a freshman philosophy class for decades. I walked for an hour along Conduit Avenue and whatever Conduit Avenue became until I hit Forest Park. I felt a little more relaxed and had no desire to go through the park at dark, so I jumped on the J train, switched trains in Williamsburg, and stood in the lobby of Dutchy's theater an hour later ready to hunt.

I tried my best not to think about Dutchy's lifeless eyes looking up at me from the small RV table and knew moving forward with my plan was the best way to keep my mind occupied and that visual at a minimum. I'd been thinking too much of my plan in terms of a heist, where I needed to assemble a team and come up with a slick plan to steal the money, but on the subway ride back, I realized it wasn't a heist, because I had no idea where the money was. Hell, I still wasn't completely convinced the money existed at all. So, I needed to become an investigator. I needed to interview witnesses and suspects and look for clues. Since I'd murdered or alienated every single person I'd come into contact with, I figured the best place to go was the base of operations for the guy who brought me into the mess.

It was surprisingly easy to get into Dutchy's theater and once I was inside, everyone seemed to remember me from the last time and didn't give me any trouble even as I snuck into his office and sat behind his desk. His computer had a password on it that I didn't think would be all that hard to break, but I was more interested in digging around his desk drawers and file cabinets. Dutchy had always been a messy kid and never took much to technology. It freaked out his paranoid nature and was one of the reasons his brief TV career hadn't turned into anything bigger. So whatever I would find that could help was going to be in a pile of paper somewhere.

That somewhere wasn't going to be his office though. I came up completely empty. Well, maybe not completely. I found a revolver with three bullets in it in a trash can. One of the pieces of junk mail that had been balled up and covering the gun was a delivery invoice with what I assumed was his home address on it. I was sure the gun had trouble a plenty attached to it and if I was ever caught with it I'd be in serious trouble, but I thought the risk was worth it in exchange for the security. I tried tucking it into the waistband of my jeans, but it kept falling into my pants and down my pant leg. The last thing I wanted was to kill my own damn self with a gunshot to the crotch from a dropped gun. The weather was too warm for there to be any jackets lying about to steal and hide the gun in, but that did give me another idea. I tucked the gun in my back pocket as snug as it would go, made sure my T-shirt covered it, then went looking for the costume shop. I'd hoped to get in and out with something functionable as a holster while avoiding contact with any other people, but the place was a disorganized fiasco of epic proportions. While I slowly spun around looking for any sort of useful gear, I felt a tap on my shoulder.

"I didn't think you were really going to do it," a gravelly female voice said from behind me.

I turned to face a short, ropey woman with graying hair and bulbous features who was feeling up my arms. She was wearing a tank top and a flowing crepe material skirt, both of which showed off an elaborate network of vibrant tattoos.

"Excuse me?"

"Dutchy said you'd get it and find it funny," she said, moving on to patting down my shoulders. "But man, it just seems mean to me."

"Right," I said, trying to buy time while I waited to see if I could figure out what was going on. "Dutchy was an ass."

"Was?"

Shit.

"You know, back when we were kids. We grew up together."

"Hmph," she said. "All the boys I grew up with were asses. Hated every last one of them. Are you an ass too?"

I looked at her steel gray eyes and tried to lock onto something I could work with. She wasn't giving me any openings.

"Lately I have been," I said. "Long time lately, I guess. But I was a good kid. Back when. You know."

"Mmmmm," she said. I took that as progress.

"So this role, it comes with a costume?"

She smiled and blushed. "Like I said, I didn't think you were going to go for it, so I didn't really think at all about how we could make it work with, you know, like public decency stuff around here."

Oh, I didn't like the sound of that at all.

"I'm sure I'm going to regret this," I said.

She cut me off with a wave before I could finish, disappearing behind a curtain in the back corner furthest away from me. She returned a few seconds later holding out a neon pink fanny pack. I didn't get the joke and figured it was just another lie Dutchy told people about us, but I did think the fanny pack would make a great holster for the revolver in my back pocket. She blushed again as I took the fanny pack from her and buckled it around my waist.

"It's certainly tacky," I said. "And I don't get whatever joke Dutchy was referring to, but I don't see how anyone could find this thing indecent."

"They will when it's all that you're wearing."

Oh.

Chapter Nine

The gun fit perfectly in the fanny pack and I didn't care how I looked. My nasty mood and posture surely painted me as less of a target than the average tourist and, again, I harbored a secret hope that some punk would try and mug me and I'd have an excuse to let loose. But I made the three-block walk to the address on Dutchy's invoice safely. Even though the street-level business was a mailbox drop store, I didn't think anything of it at first and looked around for a buzzer or a stairwell to the apartments above. But there was no buzzer. There were no apartments. The delivery invoice address *was* the mailbox store.

I crumpled the invoice and threw it on the ground in disgust and briefly thought about rushing into the store, gun drawn, and pistol-whipping the clerk until he gave up Dutchy's home address. That freaked me out even more than some of the other horrible things I'd done because it was the first time I'd thought about hurting someone innocent just to get something I needed. Something I *wanted*. I felt like Gollum in *Lord of the Rings* with the gun as my precious. It was changing me by playing on the worst parts of my personality and the worst parts of my heart's evil desires. I should have dumped it in the first garbage can I found and thrown the bullets down a drain, but I twisted the belt of the fanny pack around so the gun was closer to my hands and walked away, thinking about what I could do next.

I took three steps away from the store and looked back once more to see if anything about the way the clerk acted through the window was enough to make me okay with going after him. Bianca Dade went into the store and talked to the clerk briefly before coming back out and walking my way. It didn't take long though to realize the woman approaching me, then passing me, wasn't Bianca. But it did remind me that I'd been so focused on Dutchy and the money that I hadn't put in any real effort in hunting down Bianca to get my stuff back. It was time to change that.

Still without a phone or computer access, I made my way back to the cyber café I'd done my earlier research in and jumped online to see what I could find out about Ms. Bianca Dade. I'd always suspected that was a stage name and a quick search on Facebook only made that case stronger. But it was all I had, so I plugged her name in Google along with actress and had better results. She worked steadily as an actress in small roles at small theaters, and her name came up plenty of times in show lists and occasionally was paired with a headshot. None of that helped me find her real name though, which was what I would need to have any hope of finding her address.

I finally caught a lucky break when I found her name in the cast of a performance of the musical *Hairspray*. Each cast member's professional headshot was paired with their high school yearbook photo. I copied Bianca's photo into the Google image search and got a hit on a newspaper article about her arrest at age seventeen for breaking into a neighbor's house.

Real name: Angela Bianca Retzinger.

That was the perfect kind of name to plug into the online white pages with confidence that whatever address comes up is the one you're looking for. The address was two blocks away from the mailbox store and I was happy to walk by this time with no thought of assaulting the clerk.

Bianca's building was a glass and steel monster that stuck out from the trash heaps and scrap yards around it like a giant gentrification beacon calling for trust fund kids and professional couples looking to slum in Queens but still keep the amenities of a Manhattan pad. Her dad was a Secret Service agent, which wouldn't have been salary enough for an apartment in a building like that for himself, let alone for his daughter. So I was getting a vague idea of how he might have come to be indebted to my ex-wife's family. Though considering Bianca's own larcenous tendencies, I wouldn't be surprised to hear she had done something shady on her own to lease it.

Listen to me, the pot calling the kettle rotten.

I stood off to the side by the front door debating how to get by the security. Movies had led me to believe all I had to do was wait for some nice soul to go in first and hold the door for me if it was just a buzzer, but I had a harder time recalling tips on getting by professional doormen. The easy thing to do would be to give my name to the doorman and wait for him to call up to her apartment and tell her I was waiting for her, but then the easy thing for her would be to find any one of the other exits out of the building where I couldn't see her and leave me stupid and waiting.

So I waited. Whether I was stupid or not can be left to history to decide.

There was a Starbucks across the street that I could have camped out in and kept watch from while waiting for Bianca to show herself, but I knew the chances of me falling asleep while waiting were pretty high, if not damn near certain. It was settled then—I'd give my name to the doorman and roll the dice.

But there was no doorman. There was a security booth with no one behind it. I was halfway to the back of the lobby and the elevator when I felt a tug in my conscience and looked back. Something was off. When I leaned over the security desk, I found a blocky man in a white suit tied up and gagged. The way his head lolled off to the side, I assumed he'd been knocked out. His chest was still rising and falling with the twitches of life, so I looked around for something to cut him loose with. I didn't see anything, then realized that if someone had gone to the trouble to tie up the doorman, they weren't just delivering a secret balloon bouquet. I shrugged apologetically to the doorman and promised him I'd come back to help him after I checked in on Bianca.

He was still knocked out, so he didn't respond, but I felt better. I had the good sense to wait until I was alone in the elevator to pull the gun out of my fanny pack but couldn't put enough common sense into play to just walk away. The gun was small enough to keep relatively hidden against my leg as I made my way down the hallway to Bianca's door which, guessing from the way the doors were spaced, would be smack in the middle of the hall.

I kept the gun against my leg when I knocked with

the other hand. Nobody came to the door, so I knocked again. I jiggled the door handle to see if it was unlocked. It wasn't. I knocked again, louder and angrier this time. This time someone opened the door just enough to peek out at me and I shot him in the head. The sound was excruciatingly loud in such a tight space and I briefly freaked out and froze, until the door began closing from the weight of the corpse pushing against it. I used my shoulder to push my way through and heard the wall next to me explode, adding to the shrill echoing in my head from the first gunshot.

There were only two more bullets left in my gun, so I couldn't blindly shoot away. That meant my only option was to zig and zag through the apartment until I had a better sense of what was going on. Bianca was having none of that and by the time I found her, she was on top of another guy strangling him with her bound hands.

"We should probably leave when you're done," I yelled over the ringing in my head. "Those shots were really loud."

She nodded and quickly finished off the guy underneath her. I went to the kitchen and got a pair of meat scissors from a cutting block next to the faucet so I could cut the plastic cuffs off her hands. I was about to put the knife back when I remembered the doorman downstairs.

"We can go out through the garage," she said, snapping a picture with her cell phone of the guy she'd strangled. "I have a car."

"Is my stuff still in the glovebox?"

"Probably. Why are you taking the scissors?"

"Gun only has two more bullets and the doorman needs to be cut loose."

"Cops can cut the doorman loose, and who are you

really going to stab before they can shoot you first?"

I followed her to the same car I had arrived in just a few days ago but might as well have been a decade ago for as much as I'd seen…and done.

All my stuff was indeed still in the glovebox and I was relieved to the point of tears when I grabbed it all. My phone felt sturdy and powerful in my pocket. My wallet bestowed a sense of security and safety I hadn't felt since I arrived. I gave her the address of the Comfort Inn and approached the front desk triumphantly with my ID and my debit card and asked for a room.

The clerk took my card, smiled, swiped it, then returned it to me like it had cut her.

"I'm sorry that card's been declined."

I'd been poor enough for long enough that every time I swiped a card, I held my breath, waiting for the inevitable decline and wondering which of my myriad excuses I'd use to save face. And it was always embarrassing, and frustrating. Even knowing I had enough in my bank account to cover a month of stays at the hotel, the residual embarrassment was strong, and I faded back away from the counter, not even bothering with excuses.

"What a moron," Bianca said, hip-checking me out of the way. "Why do you keep using the expired cards when I put the new ones right on the counter?"

"Uh?"

"Men? Am I right?"

The clerk nodded in agreement and took the card that Bianca offered.

"My husband could have the right card in his wallet and still find a way to pull out the expired card," the clerk said, swiping the card.

Bianca turned and winked at me, then took the keys

and waved for me to follow her.

"Do you need some help with your luggage?"

Bianca waved off the clerk with another smile. So many smiles. Smiles that were making me uncomfortable in ways I hadn't been uncomfortable since the early days of my relationship with my late wife.

"We didn't bring any luggage," Bianca said. "Clothes don't figure much into our travel plans, if you know what I mean?"

Chapter Ten

My late wife, Posey Wade, made an impression on me early in our time together in grad school in Detroit by paying for a round of drinks I had ordered but been unable to pay for after my card was declined. That was back in the days when I didn't have any money and would swipe my card hoping that money would magically appear to cover whatever nonsense I'd intended to buy. And somehow something almost always happened to cover my tab.

Back then I'd felt entitled enough about myself to assume the universe was taking care one of its most valuable citizens. Now I was smart enough to realize every one of those moments had been another cursed IOU against my soul, building on my curse of survival. The fact the money sitting in my account was blood money inherited from my wife's family against their wishes after I'd shot her to death in self-defense only fueled the creepy feeling building in my mind about what Bianca was up to.

She swiped the card for our room, a suite from the looks of the expansive foyer, and stepped aside for me to enter first. It had every surface indication of being nothing more than a polite gesture, but I couldn't help my skepticism.

"Sending me in first to test for traps?" I asked, with no sense of irony whatsoever.

There were no traps, but there was only one bed. It would be nice to be in a situation where this small thing was the extent of our conflict and it could be the meet-cute that started us off on a charmed romantic comedy existence. In reality, it was one more headache in a situation that was bound to get worse before offering both of us a series of impossible choices.

"My wife and I had a cute meeting back in the day," I said, flopping into the lounge chair next to the bed. "She paid for a round of drinks I'd offered to buy for her and her friends when my card was declined."

Bianca nodded and pulled off her T-shirt.

"She had a problem with sex," I continued. "Not with the mechanics, or the pleasure of it, you know? She had a problem with boundaries."

Another nod. Buttons of her jeans unsnapped, wiggling her hips a bit to pull them down.

"I'm a bit of a moron about it all, frankly. Never much for sex myself. But I fell hard for her and the more we fooled around, the deeper I fell under her control. That put me in a weird spot where I never could tell if she really loved me or if she was just trying to use me."

"I get that," she said.

I waited for her to take something else off but she didn't.

"I suspect it was a combination of both," I said. "There was a part of her that really did love me. I want to believe that. I *have* to believe that. But I was a different guy with her. More naïve."

Bra. Pop.

"I can see that," she said.

"Everything changed though," I said, pulling the gun out of my fanny pack, "when I killed her."

"Jesus Christ," she said, grabbing her clothes and running into the bathroom. "You're a fucking lunatic."

"Says the woman who held me up at gunpoint and took all my shit my first time in the city."

"This is a revenge thing? Jesus. You're a twisted—"

"I don't have the energy for revenge anymore," I said. "I just wanted you to know my story. Why I'm here. Who I am. What I do."

"Mmmmm," she said.

She didn't say anything for a few minutes and then I heard the toilet flush and she came out with her clothes back on. I popped open the gun, something I'd been practicing while she was in the bathroom, dropped the remaining two bullets on the floor, and put the gun back in the fanny pack.

"I'm over it," I said. "Seeing my stuff in your glove-box was very cathartic. But it's time to move on. Move forward."

"Start by telling me why you're here. Why you're *really* here."

"Reality. Huh. That one's a bit...twisty. Surface reality: Dutchy brought me here to help him find the missing money from the theater, and I was going to use it to get out of town for good and go off the grid."

"And the real reality?"

"I needed to get away. Everywhere I looked there were reminders of my wife or her family. They hate me. I couldn't take it."

"And if you got the money, right now, what would you do with it?"

"Diversified mix of aggressive stocks, big cap stuff, a few foreign offerings, and some bonds for stability."

She smiled and eased up close to me, rubbing herself against my chest.

"What would you *really* do with all that money?"

I leaned into her ear and whispered, "I'd cash out every dollar that came from that family and litter their corpses with it after I killed them all."

She pushed me away and her look was sour. I expected her to hit me or leave or pull a knife or something out of her pocket, but she nodded instead and went to the desk to grab a pen and pad of paper.

"Okay, then," she said. "I know where the money is."

"That seems too easy."

"It is."

"Then why haven't you taken it before now?"

"Never had a good reason before now."

"I'm a good reason?"

"Narcissistic motherfucker. I don't care about you but the guys you want to take out killed my dad. I want to roll in that money when you drop it on their bodies and shove it down their lifeless goddamn throats."

My kind of girl.

"So where is it?"

"You tell me, college boy. Said you went to grad school. Ever read 'The Purloined Letter'?"

"Shit. I thought about that. It makes sense. Not as, like, any kind of literary homage, most people are too stupid for that, but what most people *are* is lazy."

"Best place to hide money taken out in a fake mortgage on a building where nobody is going to think to look for it?"

"The same goddamn building?"

"Not even in a safe," she said. "It's kind of a pain to get to, so you won't stumble on it trying to clean the heater or whatever, but if you know where to look for it, easy-peasy."

"And you know where to look for it?"

Now I got the smile again.

"I'm the one who hid it."

"Let's go get it then," I said, a little too excitedly.

I was bouncing on the tips of my feet and did my best not to grab her and kiss her in an emotional blast that would only make things more awkward.

"Fine," she said, agreeing a little too easily. "We go get it right now. Big bag of money. Then what? You can't get on a plane because you don't have your driver's license so we'd have to—"

"I do though. My wallet was in your glovebox so—"

"Your credit cards and license are gone. Dutchy made me get rid of them right away so you couldn't run away."

"Because he lured me here under bullshit pretenses," I said. "Doesn't matter though. I can get a new one when I get back home and you have one, right, because you were driving an Uber, even if it was a fake one, so I don't see what the problem is."

"So we roll into town, Detroit, Michigan, with your wife's family waiting for you and Cristal coming at you from the back end. Maybe even waiting there for you too because he can get on a plane and you can't. Are you ready, right then, for your war?"

"Ex-wife," I said, knowing I sounded pedantic, but trying to buy more time to come up with a good answer.

"He checks on that money damn near every day.

Likes to hold it and rub up on the bag like it's a hot single girl at a bar. He'll know it's gone the day we take it and he'll come for us."

I nodded and wobbled on my feet now with my previous bouncing enthusiasm sapped by reality. She had a point and I had an issue on my hand. My revenge had always been in my head, in my soul, but never in the real world. I had always assumed that fate would intervene somehow and things would get done or I'd die. Win-win. For me at least.

"Working with me," I said, "can be kind of a hazard though. Like, almost everyone I work with ends up dead and at least two of them I killed myself."

"You didn't seem all that dangerous begging for mercy when I held you up."

I shrugged. "I didn't beg for mercy. I was pissed. And you saw it, the real me, when I pulled the gun on you in the bathroom. Do you want to risk being with...that...when times get desperate?"

"We're talking about murder. Robbery, lying, assault, and murder. Premeditated murder. You don't bring in Boy Scouts for that kind of shit."

"I did my part by warning you. Whatever else happens...well, whatever."

"Such a wordsmith. Now why don't we lie down, have a rest, and when we wake up, we can figure out what we're going to do and how we're going to do it."

I patted the bed. "No funny business?"

"The last time I took my clothes off in front of you I had a gun pulled on me."

I was back to bouncing on my feet. She'd started bouncing too. I was still uncomfortable with what we were talking about and couldn't see a way forward. I'd done awful things and I knew I would do awful things again, but the only reason I didn't put a gun to my head and end it all was a fear of the unknown in the afterlife, and the desire for my awful deeds to be done in the path of something at least resembling good.

I'd never planned on killing Dutchy. I definitely hadn't planned on killing Posey, and I clung tight to that because it was all I had when I tried to convince myself I wasn't an awful person. And whether she believed me or not, Bianca was in danger working with me and that made me incredibly uncomfortable. So I told her I wanted to go sit in the hot tub instead of taking a nap and left her in the room while I went to Dutchy's theater to look for the money on my own.

Chapter Eleven

After I graduated from college the first time, I bypassed the lure of steady employment and decent earnings for a string of crappy temp jobs. One of the best of that lot was the year or so I worked as a theater technician for a children's theater. I built sets, worked the lights and sound, and learned how to use a nail gun. It was the most masculine year of my life, but the one part of it that I'd never been able to conquer was working the fly system.

I'd never been particularly afraid of heights, but working a fly system—the system of cables, weights, cobbled together ropes, and wires that brought the sets and, occasionally, actors, onto the stage—is not just being way up high. Ridiculously high. It's being way up high and needing to hang over the edge to pick up and move heavy weights. It's being way up high and needing to stand on one foot and stretch unnaturally far to get a stuck light gel changed out. It's putting yourself into a position no body was ever meant to be in and just thinking about it made me sweaty and nauseated. But it was the only place I could think of in a theater to hide money that was both easy to access and virtually impossible to discover.

No one in the theater must have known about what happened to Dutchy or, more importantly, that I had been responsible for it, because I had free run of the place to snoop around backstage and up in the catwalks for the best place to hide money. I found the spot right about the time someone found me.

"Took you for a pussy up here so high," Cristal Hate said from behind me.

"I've survived as long as I have by playing to people's low expectations of me."

"I said you was a pussy, not a moron."

I was going dizzy trying to keep one eye on Cristal and the other on a loose heater grate just out of arm's reach where I thought the money was likely to be hidden. And with Cristal standing in front of me with his most intimidating look shooting my way, I was even more convinced I was in the right spot. Until he pulled a long black rod from behind his back that looked like it had come from the fireplace set of a medieval castle. Maybe I was nowhere near the money and this was the best place for him to come to kill me.

Finally.

I flexed my fingers and wiggled out the tension in my back. Cristal bounced on his toes a few times before stepping backward a bit. Dutchy's gun was still in my fanny pack and I was mentally calculating the time it would take me to unzip the fanny pack, pull the gun, aim, and fire, and if all that could happen before he ran me through with his giant poker.

"Always weird being up here," I said, trying to gauge what I could of his intentions. "Such a weird place with heights and heavy weights all around."

Cristal jumped twice and swung the rod in his hands.

"Don't care about heights," he said, "And I can bench three-fifty so not worrying about heavy weights either."

I nodded. Watching his movements. Looking for the trigger switch.

"You gonna poke me with that stick of yours?"

"Not like I want to or anything. Just looking out for my business."

"Mmmmm," I said. "Business. Right. 'Cause I'm going to reach up into that vent and pull out a bag full of money you stole and take it back home with me."

"You gonna try."

I reached for the vent and came up just a little short so I tried to stretch harder but there was no way I was going to reach it with just my arms.

"Don't suppose you want to give me a boost," I said, half laughing, trying to diffuse my embarrassment.

He didn't offer a boost, but he did hold out his big iron rod.

"I got these long-ass arms and I still can't reach in there. That's kinda the point, so I use this."

He pushed it into my hand. I had no idea what was going on but I took the rod anyway. As I used the rod to poke into the vent and hook the bag, I realized what was going to happen. He'd set me up to steal his money with a big stick that could also be used as a weapon when he shot me dead and claimed self-defense. I'd been so focused on looking for the moment to justify my desire to take him out that I hadn't thought about him setting me up.

So this was how it would end. Way up higher than I ever wanted to be with my arms over my head and enough money to change my life tantalizingly close. I pulled the bag out of the vent and waited for the shot. A shot that never came. Cristal was smiling when I set the bag down.

"I can see it in your eyes," he said. "The hate. The darkness. You want to kill so badly. But you don't have the burning yet. You don't have the trigger."

"The hell you mumbling about?"

"Take it. Ain't worth me dying for it," he said, sounding far calmer and wiser than I would have expected. "I'll make that in a bad week round here these days."

"In the theater?"

"No, not in the theater. Jesus, you're a dumbass. Just doin' what I do. My business."

"Your business…"

"It keeps me from the trigger, man. You need to sort out your own business before you—"

"I strangled Dutchy to death and left him in a trailer."

"And you came here to do the same to me?"

"I came here for the money."

He nodded to the bag at my feet. "I said you could take it."

"I don't trust you."

"And I don't give a fuck what you think of me. Take the bag or don't but get outta my building and go sort your shit out."

"And you won't come after me?"

"You'd like that, wouldn't you? Have me sneak up on you and give you a chance to wrap them soft white hands round my own neck. Well fuck that. You want to kill me you gonna have to work at it like everyone else. You wanna find an easy kill, go stab a bum at the bus station."

I handed him back the iron poker and walked away with the duffel bag slung over my shoulder. When I checked it outside, I half expected to find it full of phone books or play money or something like that, but the money was there and it was real. And I was tweaked up on adrenaline expecting a kill shot that never came. I scratched the back of my head and walked toward the bus station.

Part of me wondered if I should stop off at Bianca's house and show her the money and split it with her or whatever. But I knew that was my emotions smacking me around because it was really the worst thing I could do for her. With my luck, she'd want to come with me back to Detroit and first thing off the bus we'd be ambushed. I'd survive and she'd be dead, and I'd have another ghost haunting my dreams and my afterlife. And if she did survive, I'd be stuck with a tagalong when I needed to focus on figuring out what I was going to do with my wife's family.

Thinking about revenge made me squirm. I shifted the bag of money back and forth on my shoulder as I walked toward the subway. I stopped at the next intersection and turned around back toward the hotel. As I walked, my arms swung widely, and I realized how healthy and active I was being. Healthy and active had never been my style, but somehow being in New York City made walking easier. Back in Michigan I had trouble mustering the enthusiasm to walk to the end of my apartment complex to check the mail, but in this city I didn't think anything of walking ten blocks in one direction then turning around and walking ten more in the other direction on a whim. Carrying a bag full of money.

Bianca swung at me when she opened the door, but I

dodged it easily. She surely saw me through the peephole, so when she opened the door, I knew she hadn't completely written me off, but I knew she'd still be pissed. I threw the bag on the bed and flopped down after it.

"I'm taking it back to Detroit with me," I said, "and wondered if you wanted to come with me."

She looked at me with her mouth open and her eyes narrowed as she unzipped the bag and rifled through it.

"How did you..."

"It wasn't hard to figure out," I said. "I just put myself in Dutchy's dumbass head and thought about where I'd have to be too stupid or scared to look for the money under my own goddamn nose."

"And you just took it."

"Then dropped it here for you. Well, at you. It's not yours. I guess."

"Jesus. When Cristal finds out he's going to—"

"He found me when I was taking it. I thought he was going to kill me."

"Jesus," she said again. "Jesus Christ. What did you do?"

"He threatened me a bit, psychologically, you know, not physically. And then he let me go."

"Just let you go? With his money?"

I held my arms out and shrugged broadly.

"Bullshit. What did you do to him?"

"Nothing. I swear. I was tweaked up and really wanted to...I mean I had my gun, I had this revolver from Dutchy's desk ready to go and I was waiting for him to make his move. And he never did."

She zipped the bag up and stepped back from it.

"This is crazy. There's something you're not telling me."

"I don't have the attention span for a lie like that. It's the truth. It's like he knew what was going on in my head and was messing with me. Daring me to kill him."

"But you didn't?"

"I'm not a monster. I don't think. Not yet."

She nodded but stayed away from the bag.

"Okay. Don't fucking lie to me next time. That's bullshit and I don't do bullshit."

"You robbed me the first time we—"

"I don't do regrets either. That grade A toxic bullshit and I just can't. So Detroit. I have a car. You still want to stick to your stupid bus plan?"

"Your Uber car?"

"Fuck you. I can't do this. I don't care how much I hate those assholes. I'll work on my own."

I picked up the bag and made it all the way out onto the sidewalk before I came to terms with the fact that I really didn't want to ride a bus all the way back to Detroit and retreated to Bianca. This time I didn't dodge her punch and took it right in the balls. I doubled over and threw up, suddenly feeling better than I had in quite a while. I'd been playing the tough guy for too long and it had been wearing on me. I worked better as a victim and being underestimated. Throwing up all over that hotel room floor brought that nature back for me, and I was ready to roll.

We didn't bother trying to clean up the mess, Bianca just took a hundred-dollar bill from the bag and left in on the dresser for the housekeeping staff.

"I stay here a lot," she said. "And I've always wanted to do that."

I nodded, distracted by getting the bag over my shoulder without falling into the vomit on the floor. My feet didn't get the message though. I didn't fall completely in it, but I stepped through it enough to drag the chunks and the smell with me as we left.

Chapter Twelve

"You're not wearing those vomit shoes in my car," Bianca said, refusing to unlock my door.

"I'm not getting in that car without my shoes on. I still have some very strong...Jesus, just come on. Haven't I been through enough with you and this car already?"

"What you've been through in a nasty pile of your own vomit and I don't want you tracking it into the car I just paid two hundred fifty dollars to have professionally detailed."

I hesitated and danced around on my feet outside of her car before finally agreeing to leave my shoes on the street before getting in.

"I have to admit," I said about fifteen minutes later as we were cruising through the Holland Tunnel on our way to New Jersey and then Detroit, "being a passenger feels downright luxurious in stocking feet."

She sighed and grunted. We were silent for quite a while as we drove through the surprisingly hilly and rather gorgeous New Jersey landscape. I knew it was called the Garden State, in theory I guess, but I had always assumed that must have been ironic. What it turned out to be, apparently, was years and years of television and late night comedians riding a joke that wasn't true. What they should have been telling jokes about was not the smell or the sewers or whatever, but the drivers. Drivers in New Jersey suck.

They suck so bad, in fact, that New Jersey driving would be the instigator for sending me down the darkest path toward my darkest timeline. It started innocently enough at a truck stop plaza near the New Jersey/Pennsylvania border when I nodded to an Orthodox Jewish family heading out of the plaza and was almost hit by a shiny new Honda Civic with New Jersey plates. I flipped the driver off as he drove away and assumed that was the end of it. Bianca got a startling amount of Red Bull from the store. I went to pee and filled up the gas tank.

When we walked out of the plaza, the car that had almost hit me was parked next to Bianca's so close that she couldn't get in her door. Instead of making things worse, we thought, by engaging the other car, we both tried to go in through the passenger side. But Bianca couldn't get over the center console. I made a joke about her being an old lady. She punched me in the elbow and told me if I was such a smart-ass, I could drive. The car didn't follow us out of the parking lot, but I'd seen enough low budget horror movies and grindhouse noir flicks to know we weren't through with them yet.

I kept my eyes on the rearview mirror as we drove through Pennsylvania and Bianca slept. When it had been more than half an hour since we'd seen the car, I let my breath out and felt relief. Briefly. Then I felt agitated. Again. Something I'd been feeling a lot since I arrived in New York and something that the Red Bull was doing nothing to help. I was coming up on a slow moving car in the left lane and instead of tailgating it until it moved over, like I had a tendency to do, I played good driver and moved to the right lane.

When I checked my rearview mirror to make sure there were no cars in the lane I was moving into, I saw another car coming up quickly in the left lane. I took a long swing from the Red Bull can and moved my hands into the ten and twelve position I'd been taught long ago but rarely ever used. I wiggled my fingers until I felt the tension ease, then gripped the steering wheel as tightly as I could. The cruise control was on, but I tapped my foot on the gas pedal anyway, waiting to slam it to the floor.

"Don't," Bianca said the third or so time I tapped my foot.

"Sorry," I said. "Didn't think you could hear that. I tap my foot when I'm—"

"Not what I'm talking about, dude."

"What do you—"

"Let 'em pass. I can feel your temper rising all the way over here."

"I don't know what you're—"

Her eyes popped open and she sat up in her seat. "You're not Mad Max and you're not going to get us both killed because you can't—"

"Shit," I said. "They're not going to pass us."

"I told you to—"

"I'm in the right lane," I said. "What else do you want me to do?"

The car was in the right lane now and it was coming up even faster in my mirror. I couldn't tell for sure if it was the Honda from the truck stop, but I knew deep inside that it was. It had to be. Bianca turned to look out the back window and saw the same thing. She was no longer so insistent that I let them pass.

"Maybe we should pull off into the bushes or some-thing," she said. "And just let them go by."

"They'll see us. And then we'll be sitting—"

"Shit, they're going to hit us."

I moved back into the left lane and sped up. The other car did the same so I moved back into the right lane. The other car did the same. It was a Honda, the same color as the one from the truck stop, and I braced for impact. And impact that never came. The car stayed on my tail, but it didn't ram us. That pissed me off even more. I looked in the rearview mirror and saw the driver was a tall, gangly-looking middle-aged man with a greasy, shorter fella in the passenger seat. They both smiled and waved when I made eye contact with them in the mirror.

"Jesus," Bianca said. "I wonder if they're just nuts, not dangerous."

"They're nuts alright," I said. "But that doesn't mean they're not also dangerous."

"Slow down again and see if they'll pass."

I tapped my brakes twice quickly like my dad had taught me when I was first learning to drive. He'd said his dad had taught him and used the trick when he was a truck driver to give annoying tailgaters a scare. I thought it made my dad and my grandpa sound like assholes back then, and it felt like an asshole move when I did it. But I was in an asshole kind of mood. The Honda slowed down, barely, but didn't pass. That's when I wiggled my hips to feel the security the fanny pack, and the gun inside it, before slamming on my brakes. The Honda came screaming up behind me quickly and I waited for the impact that never came. After wobbling a bit and then spinning in a half circle, the Honda flipped high in the air before crashing spectacularly in the grass off the side of the highway.

"Oh Jesus," Bianca said. "What did you do?"

"This wasn't my—"

"Pull over. We have to go check on them."

I wiggled again. Gun still there. Fanny pack secure. So I pulled off to the side of the road and turned around to look at the wreckage, waiting for the explosion modern entertainment had assured me would come after a crash like that. But there was no explosion. There was no screaming or grinding metal sounds or anything dramatic. Just freak-ass silence and the panicked breathing of the woman sitting next to me.

"I'm going over there," I said. "Don't call anybody just yet."

"No way. That's bullshit. I don't care what you did, I don't want—"

"Just shush and keep an eye out for anything weird."

I got out of the car and walked slowly, cognizant of each and every step I took, toward the wreckage. As I got closer, I could hear hissing and groaning sounds. There looked to be two figures moving around in the car, so I hadn't killed anybody. Was I relieved? I unzipped the fanny pack and moved closer toward the car.

"Hello," I said. "Are y'all okay in there?"

There was more hissing and muffled sounds that sounded like yelling, then less muffled sounds that sounded more like "motherfucker." I stopped walking and looked back at Bianca. She had her phone in her hand but didn't seem to be talking to anyone yet. Which gave me more options. I thought back to my moment at the theater with Cristal and the gun and the money. Waiting for a moment that never came. Not quite ready, or wanting, to make the first move. I wondered if I'd have to wait here as well. The cursing was hopeful.

Finally, there was a crunching noise, followed by the driver's side door opening enough for one of the people in the car to wriggle out and stand up. He was shorter than me by a few inches, and broader in the shoulders and chest. His hair was thick and curly and sticking out all over the place. Despite the carnage of the car behind him, he didn't seem to be injured beyond a few scrapes and a slight limp as he came toward me.

Shit.

"Motherfucker," he said, completely unmuffled this time.

"I guess we both had a bit of—"

"*You* ran *me* off the road, you fucking lunatic."

"I didn't run you off of anything. I applied my brakes in a manner I've been trained—"

I think he punched me first. I need to believe he punched me first. I would tell everyone that asked after the fact that he punched me first. But as it happened, it seemed like he punched me and I shot him at the same time.

He grabbed his stomach and stumbled backward before falling to his knees. I kept my gun pointed at him in case he tried to come at me again, but he didn't. The other person in the car still hadn't emerged and I had no interest in waiting for another witness, so I ran back to the car and got in. Bianca still had her door open and her legs outside the car with her cell phone in her hand. From what I could tell, she hadn't called anyone on it yet.

"I don't want to drive away with your door open," I said. "But we're not exactly awash in time, if you know what I mean."

She nodded slowly and drew her legs back into the car slowly and, finally, closed her door slowly. I didn't see it happen, but it felt like she moved away from me as I pulled her car back out onto the highway.

"It's not my gun," I said. "So it can't be traced back to me. I don't think. Though if they go back and trace it back to Dutchy they can probably figure out I took it, especially if they talk to Cristal. But how would they get back to Dutchy? I think we're good."

I waited a few seconds to see if Bianca would say anything.

"We're good, right?"

She nodded. Slowly.

"Not that it matters anyway," I said, a few more miles down the road. "The cops are the least of our...the least of my worries."

We drove again in silence for an hour, passing through the blandest part of the state visible from the highway with no more excitement.

"You warned me," Bianca said. "So this is my fault. I have to just—"

"What are you babbling about? What did I warn you about?"

"You. And...this. What you did back there."

"Oh. Right. I just, I've seen what happens around me and it always seems like it'd be better if nobody followed me or was near me or even knew me, I guess."

"But I wanted to come anyway."

"Because of your dad."

"You're still going to kill them, right? That's what this is all about. You're getting up your nerve to kill them. Because they're not going to come at you or give you an out. Right? Tell me that's what this is and not that I've gone in with a serial killer. Or a wannabe serial killer."

Jesus. Her words cut right to places I wanted to avoid thinking about. But of course she was right. Or she was right for what she thought I was going to do. But I'd been thinking about something different. Something she probably wouldn't like. So there was no way in hell I was going to mention that to her right then. But I did it anyway. Because I'm an idiot. Or I was trying to be a good guy. Good...ish. As good as I'm capable of being.

"I was thinking," I said. "About what you said. About killing them."

This time she didn't move slowly. She was quick and nasty in her movements as she slapped at my face.

"Don't you dare," she said. "Don't you *dare* bail on me."

"I'm not bailing on you. I still need you, actually, for this to work. But I think we can do some good while we take these assholes down."

"I don't want to do good. This isn't a charity ride. I came with you, bought in to your...whatever you have going on in your life...for one purpose. To take down the people who killed my dad. To put a gun to someone's head, tell them who I am, and pull the trigger."

I was proud of myself when I held my tongue long enough to avoid mentioning her dad had killed himself and that there was likely no one single person responsible for pushing him to it. No good would come from that conversation so I stayed remarkably quiet. She kept talking, nothing in what she said registering anything inside of me, so I nodded in a few spots that seemed appropriate and let her vent.

We switched places once, when I got too tired to drive and started swerving toward oncoming traffic, and before long we were in Michigan heading toward Detroit. I briefly felt ready for my destiny and what was needed to face off against my wife's family until we were pulled over and thrown into a Department of Corrections van.

Chapter Thirteen

When you think about criminal organizations infiltrating law enforcement, you think police, FBI, sheriff's department, something like that, right? My wife's family saw beyond the vanity of that and spent decades building a thoroughly corrupt network within the Michigan Department of Corrections. This gave her uncles, her stepbrothers, and some particularly nasty cousins full run of the state's prisons and parole system, which turned out to be a pretty great way to keep a criminal enterprise running.

Until the state started privatizing more and more of it, each new contractor squeezing out a piece of the empire until it was less of an empire and more of a power core. But the Taylor family still swung enough power in the right places to make my life hell. And now I was bumping along handcuffed and hooded in the back of one of their vans. My mouth was free and I debated talking to Bianca, but I sensed she was overwhelmed by the sudden turn of events and there wasn't much I could say that would make anything better.

So we rode. In silence. Awkward, awkward silence.

When we finally stopped, it was only a few seconds between stopping and the back doors opening. I felt someone grab my arm and pull me out of the van, not concerning themselves at all with my safety as I tumbled out, smacking my legs and arms on the van and the ground. In a rare bout of good luck though, I felt no urge to vomit while my hood was still on. In fact, even when they pulled my hood off, I didn't feel sick. I felt pissed. Vindictive, certainly. But not sick. I was ready.

They pulled my mask off in a room I recognized. Jay Taylor was a guy I had once been afraid of and once tried to convince to be a source for a book I wanted to write about his family. My wife's family. Step-family. Sort of.

"Jesus Christ," I said, when I realized where I was and who I was talking to. "Why the hood if you were going to bring me somewhere I've been before and if you were going to be…well, you, who I've seen before?"

"Welcome home, Dominick."

Bianca looked at me when Jay said that in a way that echoed my own feelings about how creepy it sounded. She opened her mouth but didn't say anything. Home, as he referred to it, was the Detroit Detention Center. A boxy brick complex that used to be a correctional facility before the DOC shut it down. A few of the buildings had been reopened a few years ago under an agreement with the Detroit Police Department that converted the place into a sort of Ellis Island for criminals in Detroit. Anyone arrested anywhere in the city for any crime, was first run through the Detroit Detention Center for processing before being arraigned or kicked out to one of the other overcrowded and understaffed jails in the city. It also served as the home base for what was left of the Taylor family's empire.

"You brought a friend," Jay said. "Interesting."

"I want to believe you aren't trying to kill me," I said, feeling less confident as each word dropped from my chapped lips. "But the evidence so far leads me to believe—"

"Still as chatty as ever. Never understood how Posey put up with that. Wouldn't let anybody else get away with that shit, but you…we sometimes wonder if she really did love you."

I jumped from my chair and dove at him, realizing as I tried to swing for a punch that my hands were still cuffed behind my back. Didn't matter. I dropped my shoulder and dug into his gut as I plowed forward, sending him skidding backward and over the plastic table he'd been leaning against. When he made his way up from the floor, he was smiling. I was shaking off a cramp in my shoulder.

"Don't fucking talk about my wife like that."

"The wife you shot? The *pregnant* wife you shot?"

"You know that baby was bullshit and—"

This time it was his turn to overreact, but instead of running into me, he slugged me low in the gut and took away every last bit of wind I had in me.

"When the grunting and pissing is over," Bianca said, way too calmly for the situation, "can we get to the reason we're all here?"

Jay smiled again and held his hand out to help me up. I ignored the macho urge to wave him off and took his hand.

"Your friend is right," Jay said. "We should probably talk about why you're here."

"I don't think you want to know why we're here," I said. "You know, in Detroit, not right here this moment

103

because that wasn't really part of our plan."

"That push, that's what I was hoping for when I brought you here. It means you might have a way out of this."

"This, being?"

"My debt. My family's debt. Your *wife's* debt."

He looked directly at Bianca when he said wife.

"Talk then," I said.

"Not yet," Jay said. "This feels weird. Unprofessional. We're discussing grave matters. We should be discussing them over an adult meal in a proper environment."

I'm sure Bianca was thinking he was talking about a fancy restaurant, but I knew exactly where he wanted to have dinner and I didn't like it one bit.

"I've always liked Olive Garden," I said. "And considering your speech seems ripped from some sort of B-list Godfather guidebook, why not use a B-list Godfather setting?"

Jay sucked through his teeth and rolled his eyes at me. He never respected me, and I never cared because I knew that I irritated him in a way that no one else ever could and that was my secret weapon. But if I really was going to do some good with this situation, I couldn't piss him off too much. I needed him to keep me around. I really needed him to keep Bianca around. So I demurred from my worst tendencies and tried to replicate a reasonable facsimile of a contrite adult.

"I'll send a car to your hotel at six to take you out to my dad's old house. We'll have dinner and wine, and then we'll talk about how you can redeem your worthless existence."

"You don't know where we're staying."

He sucked his teeth again, but this time he smiled and

handed me a key card for the MGM Grand Detroit.

"Enjoy yourself, gamble responsibly, and if you see any old friends, be sure to give them my best."

Before I could ask any follow up questions, Jay Taylor disappeared and a lumbering tugboat of a human, dressed in a suit that was probably custom designed for King Kong, appeared in front of us.

"I want to miss rush hour," he said.

I'd never been to the MGM Grand in either Detroit or Las Vegas. In fact, I'd never been to Las Vegas at all despite having an interest in the city that bordered on the obsessive. Outside, the Detroit location looked very much a part of its Detroit surroundings. There were several expressway ramps bordering the casino and across the street from the DTE Energy company headquarters and a park. Just down the street was the traditional Detroit scene of liquor stores, abandoned buildings, and weedy lots.

Inside, the casino was plush, gilded, and cavernous like the oldest grand dame buildings of downtown Detroit. The energy was exciting, not depressing as I'd always heard it was, and I felt the weight of wealth and hope and high-wire intensity running through me. I held Bianca's hand as we crisscrossed the floor, opening ourselves to what the location—and the night—might have to offer.

Even as I enjoyed myself though, Jay's comment about seeing old friends poked at the back of my brain. Unlike myself, who let every word formed in my head out of my mouth, Jay only spoke when he had something to say and what he had to say usually involved people dying. Was he just trying to creep me out or was there a specific person I was supposed to run into? We each dropped a couple bucks into a slot machine that didn't do anything, then headed back through the lobby area and up to our room.

Bianca took another shower. I turned the TV to CNN for background noise while I continued trying to untangle the threads of what was going on. I hadn't gotten far into my thoughts when Bianca asked me to join her.

"I don't know," I said.

I swear. It sounded romantic and chivalrous in my head. And I really wasn't sure if it was the wise thing, but as it came out of my mouth, I realized how weird it sounded.

"I mean, this is a stressful situation. I worry about consent and, you know, is it the adrenaline goofing with your brain or is it—"

Bianca appeared in the bathroom door completely naked, sparkling under the fluorescent hotel light, and she looked like Posey. I wanted to hate them both—for things they did, for things I did, for things I wanted to do—but I couldn't. I wanted to grow out of my pettiness. I wanted to grow into...

"Just go with it," she said, leaping on top of me.

So I went with it. Twice.

An hour later we were finally able to gather our wits enough to get out of bed and leave the hotel room. I took a quick shower, locking the bathroom door behind me, and let the burn of the water cleanse me of the dirtiness (and exhilaration) I felt and pound out the knots the sex hadn't been able to release.

As I looked through the hotel room closet for an iron to clean up my wrinkled T-shirt, I noticed someone had left two garment bags in the closet. It wasn't a stretch to assume Jay had left them both to put us in his debt for the gifts as well as letting us know he could still get into the room any time he wanted.

"Pretty," Bianca said, throwing her garment bag onto the bed and holding a black cocktail dress up to her dirty clothes. "What's in yours?"

"That damn family has been trying to get me into sport coats since they met me."

Which was true, but the blazer in the garment bag was the coolest I had ever seen and made me feel like the man I imagined I might become one day. It was blue, and from a distance looked like any other blue blazer you'd see on a Ralph Lauren wannabe, but if you looked up close, you could see that there were outlines of ducks alternating with hunting hats.

It's no secret to anyone who knows me—and, frankly, to most strangers who encounter me—that I adore *Catcher in the Rye*. But Posey got the worst of my obsession, and I chose to ignore the crass, threatening possibilities in the clothing choice and believe that it was a gift Posey had gotten me that her family was finally passing along to its rightful owner. In fact, the jacket stunned me so much, I didn't even mind wearing it with the ugly pants and boring dress shirt they sent along with it. Bianca put her hand on my shoulder as I stared at myself in the mirror. I thought she was trying to move me out of the way until I realized I was crying.

"Every goddamn day," I said to the mirror, "there are new ways to paralyze me with conflicting emotions I feel about a woman I loved and felt justified in killing at the same time."

"Maybe we should skip dinner."

"It has to end sometime," I said. "And I'm getting tired of running away."

She took my hand and squeezed it, then took a knife from her purse and slipped it under her dress where it disappeared into the tight curves and sparkle of the physics-defying material. Posey was beautiful in her own way, but she never cared for elegant dresses and couldn't have pulled it off if she had wanted to anyway. She was a street poet and a bounty hunter through to her core and would have shown up at the White House and the gates of Heaven in a pair of jeans and a pair of boots if given the choice.

"Lucky bouncer who gets to search you for weapons," I said.

"Wait'll you see their faces if I have to use them."

Dinner was lovely, the wine flowed freely, and an hour into my visit, Jay asked me if I would go to a casino north of Flint and murder a guy who owed the family a bunch of money.

I said yes and had an extra scoop of ice cream with my pie.

Maybe it was the jacket, maybe it was the wine, but I'd gone back to Detroit to kill someone and this was as good of a way to start as any. It was certainly going to be more complicated than Jay was letting on, and it certainly wasn't going to turn out the way he hoped it would, but none of that mattered then. I switched from wine to bourbon and wondered if I'd get to see where Bianca hid the knife when we got back to the hotel.

"The jacket seems to have made you less of a moron," Jay said, running on his own alcohol-fueled chatter bender, I imagined.

I nodded, took a long sip of the scotch, and tried like hell not to say anything to ruin the mood. Bianca didn't seem to be having as much fun as I was though, and a few times seemed downright hostile to the entire evening. I couldn't imagine why until Jay stood, a bit wobbly, and offered a tour of the house.

"You can see the room where his wife almost strangled her stepfather to death," he said, smiling.

"The drive from New York was brutal," I said without standing. "And we didn't exactly get to nap at the hotel. So I think we're going to pass."

"Of course. I'll have someone from the hotel take you back."

The way he said it, that he was having someone from the hotel drive us, not one of the family guys, sent a bolt of creepiness down my spine as I stood up. But even knowing it was going to be bad when I saw the driver, I still didn't expect to see Parker Farmington standing next to the vehicle waiting for us.

Chapter Fourteen

There was no easy way to explain how weird and horrible it was that Parker Farmington was the one driving us—and that he worked at the MGM Grand casino—to Bianca, but I tried. I suspect I made it worse.

"You must be telling it wrong," she said after the first try.

"No," Parker said. "He really was that stupid. Sounds like he hasn't changed much since then."

"He sure does like to kidnap people though," she said.

"You came with me on your own," I said. "I tried to leave you in New York."

"I'm sure that's the way you told it to yourself in your head."

I flopped my head back into the soft, leathery seat of the SUV Parker was driving and looked out the tinted window at the glittering lights of the city. They were placed strategically enough to look like there was a vibrant and sustainable life force in the city beyond super rich tech billionaires from Ohio and super poor liberal hipsters from everywhere else.

I should have been freaked out and bracing for inevitable disaster, but the dialogue had slipped easily into the forced, but comfortable, rhythm I had developed with Parker over the course of our…unique…relationship. It wasn't a great situation, and I certainly wasn't stress-free, but I wasn't hating the ride, and I found that kind of amazing.

"Sounds like you also managed to keep your streak alive of finding women to hang out with you who are much better than you deserve," Parker said, pulling me out of my head and back into the conversation.

"This one I deserve," I said. "She robbed me at gunpoint and left me on the side of the road in Queens not even twenty minutes after we met."

Bianca threw her hands up in the air and sighed.

"And he'll never let me forget about it."

We all had a laugh, then I remembered where we were going and what still needed to be done.

"I assumed you being our driver was supposed to be some kind of threat," I said. "But you seem happy."

"You expected a sob story about gambling debts and a plea for you to do what Jay asked so I don't get whacked or some such nonsense?"

"I wouldn't call it nonsense, considering Jay's history, but yeah. You get the idea."

"Always trying to pitch your life to yourself as a story," Parker said. "This one was always stuck in his head imagining he was the main character in his life as an HBO prestige drama."

I assumed that last part was for Bianca, not me, and I kept quiet.

"More like a public access reality show," she said.

"Hardy har," I said with little enthusiasm or bite. "But if you're not a weaponized social threat to us, why are you playing chauffer?"

"Because I don't want you to do anything stupid."

"You might as well just drop us off here then if you're going to lecture me like an absentee dad."

He slowed down as we approached the hotel roundabout then stopped without getting out of the car. I looked over at Bianca, who seemed to catch on that something was off but didn't seem inclined to do anything about it, then at Parker, who'd twisted himself around to face me.

"You have a history of fucking up opportunities to start over," he said. "And hurting the people around you in the process."

"I'm aware of my history."

"Do this right or walk away. That's all I'm asking."

I tried to open the door for a dramatic exit scene, but he'd put the child locks on and the door wouldn't open.

"I appreciate the advice," I said. "I really do."

He came around to my door after an awkward second or two and opened it. While I stood next to him, he leaned in to talk to Bianca without opening her door.

"You can walk away," he said. "Nobody will say a thing."

I expected her to nod and let Parker drive her away, leaving me to fend for myself, but she wiggled out of her seat beat and up to the driver's seat and let herself out of the car. She came around to Parker and got into his face.

"I'm not a pawn. I'm not a sidekick. I'm not a plot device in his little fantasy. I know exactly why he's here and I know why I'm here."

She pulled her dress up to her waist, just short of showing off anything illicit, and I wondered if she was going for her knife. But she pulled a fifty-dollar bill from a band around her thigh and handed it to Parker.

"Thank you for the ride."

We had sex again the next morning. After, Bianca was lying across the bottom half of the bed on her stomach reading the comics from the hotel's free copy of the newspaper when she said, "I know what I'm getting into with you, but I can't say it doesn't make me nervous."

"I'm fucking terrified and I know what's going on in my head."

"So we're doing this?"

"If I can get some help from your people. Your dad's people."

"A plea for revenge from the daughter of a cop killed in the line of duty that could also take down one of the most corrupt law enforcement families in the state is as close to a sure thing as you'll ever get in this life or the next."

I nodded and threw a blanket over her naked body.

"We need to get to work then and I have trouble focusing on anything as is, let alone with you prancing around nude."

She sighed, rolled over onto her back, and threw her legs up into the air, then scooted toward me, wiggling her goodies the entire way.

"Is this distracting? Should we just keep screwing until it's not distracting anymore?"

"I'm serious."

"So am I," she said, flipping onto all fours and coming at me again. "This is some scary shit we're up against and it's way past normal. For Christ's sake, we barely know each other yet here we are naked in a casino hotel room paid for by your ex-wife's family where we're supposed to chill out before you catch a ride with your old professor up to another casino where you're supposed to kill a guy."

"Sounds like my life has a twisted set of writers when you put it like that."

"She grabbed me between the legs."

"We all have our ways of coping. I like to have sex and shoot stuff. Which do you want to be part of?"

I grabbed her and took her from behind. It was angry and fast and awkward. It ruined the mood she'd been building and we separated awkwardly afterward.

"Maybe we should go shoot stuff instead," I said.

She hung over the side of the bed and threw up all over the floor.

Jay thought taking us to the gun range was a good idea and arranged for a driver to pick us up. Bianca sat in the front seat and kept quite the entire drive. I don't know why I expected something different from Jay, but instead of taking us to a neutral site, he took us back to the family compound where there was a gun range under the property in the bunker complex they had built to prep for the end of the world or the end of Detroit or the end of any other part of their operation. Again, Bianca remained quiet as Jay and one of his…assistants…led us into the bowels of the complex.

The gun range was a small enclave off the combination pantry/armory.

"Seemed like a smart move at the time to keep the food and the ammo together," Jay said, when he caught me looking oddly at the mix of canned goods and bullet boxes. "But now I just get hungry every time I come down here."

"How often do you come down here? I figured you just kept it for intimidating rogue family members after you ask them to murder rogue family customers."

"You're not rogue and you're not family," Jay said. "You're a pain in the ass and I come down here every day practicing to defend myself when the shit show that follows you around comes my way again."

"Huh," I said, more hurt than I cared to admit.

Jay set up the target and a selection of handguns and automatic weapons for us to try. I stuck with handguns because, frankly, all of the guns scared me and, as Jay had so sagely mentioned, I managed to be a weapon of mass destruction just fine without needing to arm myself. As I pulled off shot after shot from a revolver the size of my forearm, I tried to add up in my head the number of people I'd killed with a gun.

I'd always remember my first: Morton Taylor, Jr.—went by the name Rickards around me for some reason—who I gunned down in a sleazy alley in downtown Toledo, Ohio right after he'd killed my dead wife's brother. And just a year ago, almost exactly to the day, I shot my wife when she tried to blow me up in a vacation home she owned but never told me about in a dying Michigan resort town. And then, a few minutes after that, I had emptied a clip from an automatic rifle into Jay's brother when he tried to run me over with a car.

Frankly, thinking about it in those terms, I was surprised Jay didn't gun me down right then. I could only imagine he had something much worse for me in mind than a quick shot to the head in a bunker gun range. The whole thing was only making Bianca's mood worse as well, if the damage she was dishing out to the poor paper targets was any indication. She'd bypassed the small handguns and elegant assault rifles for a nasty-looking sawed-off shotgun.

"From afar, it doesn't look like much," she said to Jay, while she reloaded it, "but get too close to it and it can tear your head off and blow a hole in your gut big enough to walk through."

She looked at me and winked when she said that last part. I'd love to believe it was a friendly gesture of solidarity and her hinting she had my back as we went out on our first kill together, but I read it more as a warning not to get too close and, if I did, not to make her angry. Though I suspected it may have been too late then to avoid any of that.

"That's a lovely image," Jay said, guiding me over toward where Bianca was standing, "and it's the perfect segue into another round of goodbyes. Check-in will begin shortly at your new hotel for the next few nights, so it's best you get on the road so you have some time to get settled in, maybe have a nice meal, maybe have a nice bit of...nah, it's best if we don't talk about the dirty stuff, right? Anyway—"

"I want to drive," Bianca said. "I'm a driver too and I feel like I'm getting ridden over here and we're not your slaves or anything like that. We're family...well, he's family and that makes me some kind of family friend so we can be trusted. I mean, Jesus, Dominick left, he was long gone, and he could have kept running, but he came back. He wants to do this as much as you want him to."

Jay laughed and looked at me.

"You two really do deserve each other," he said. "How about I let y'all take my car?"

"Just take us to the airport and we'll get a car from there. Thank you."

Chapter Fifteen

The only car they had bigger than a sub-compact that seemed to barely qualify as a car was a minivan and we took it. In retrospect, it was an odd kind of omen of what would happen at the hotel that would bring the whole thing crashing down around us. But at the time, all we cared about was that it was big, it was decked out in leather and fancy wood, and it was generic looking enough that we'd be harder to follow. We hoped.

"Why didn't we take your car?" I asked. "This thing makes me feel like I should change into khakis and a boring polo shirt."

"The fellas we left behind in New York know my car. Maybe it's best if we don't make ourselves too easy to find."

"I guess. But this?"

"If we're running for our lives and have to outrun the bad guys, would you rather be in this or that little motor scooter-looking car that was our only other choice?"

She had a good point.

"Since you're driving," I said, "can I crash in the back and watch a movie?"

"I need you up here to keep me awake and make it look like we're a happy couple driving instead of a vulnerable single mom."

"You sure didn't look all that vulnerable alone at the theater when you—"

"I get it, you're pissed I robbed you and left you in the street. It was a shitty thing to do, but you *have* to get past that."

"If only it were that easy," I said. "I have trouble letting stuff go. Jesus, that's why we're in the mess in the first place. An entire life of not being able to let anything go, even the little stuff."

"Considering the other things we've done together since that awkward first meeting, your degree of petty spite does seem odd."

"My wife and I did way crazier sex stuff than we've done and I shot her."

Even as the words were coming out of my mouth, I could taste the regret.

"Don't fucking joke about that Dominick."

I nodded and rummaged around the glovebox for a map. We were going to need to be as undetectable as possible for a while and that meant forgoing GPS apps for navigation. I knew the main area we'd travel toward the casino, but if anything happened to throw us off our game—and by this point it would have been negligent and borderline insane not to expect something horrible to ruin our plan—I wanted to know what our escape routes were. But there was no map.

"We should get a map the next time we stop," I said, closing the glovebox.

"Do they even make maps anymore?"

"There are still people who don't use cell phones for

119

everything," I said. "Especially out here in the boon-docks."

More driving. More quiet, though less awkward than last time. More time to think about how stupid we were for even attempting what we were thinking of doing. After a couple of hours on the road, we started seeing giant windmills pop up occasionally before overwhelming the skyline outside of a small town with a fancy football stadium. Bianca tapped my leg and exited just after we passed the elaborate blue and red stadium visible from the highway.

Every time I saw the giant windmills, I was impressed and imagined that they were giant propellers for airships or spaceships or something immense and amazing. Of course, the reality was that they were amazing, but not in my goofy science fiction way. And, according to the citizens of towns like the one we pulled into, the amazing was more than compensated for by a drastic lowering of the quality of life for those living nearby. A quality of life that included not being able to use cell phones regularly or get good cable TV due to the electromagnetic inter-ference from the wind farms. For interlopers like us though, it was the perfect place to have a conversation we didn't want to be spied on.

The exit ramp looped around once and dumped us at a T-shaped intersection. In front of us was a small truck stop set up with a gas station and an American cooking-style buffet restaurant. To the left was a long stretch of fields and farms that didn't seem to lead to much of anything else and to the right, I assumed we'd find the town. The money from the wind farm had paid for a luxurious football stadium for the high school, but it didn't seem like much else of that money had worked its way into the local economy.

The two-block downtown area had the same Rust Belt look as I'd seen in any number of towns—big and small. Storefronts that weren't boarded or covered in For Lease signs weren't the mom-and-pop antique shops and artisan bakeries HGTV would lead you to believe made up small town America. Rather, they were occupied by check cashing stores, dollar stores, no-name banks that catered to folks with sketchy credit and even sketchier job histories, and liquor stores to keep everyone lubed up when the single bar in town closed for the night.

Bianca pulled into the parking lot behind that single bar—in this town it was called Able's Body—and turned to me while she kept the engine running.

"Minivan blended in nicely on the road," she said, "but kind of sticks out like a soccer mom's sore thumb around here."

"Are you sure this is the place? The name sounds like a strip club, not a townie bar."

"Maybe it's both?"

There were no other cars in the parking lot. The clock on the dashboard showed it was after three p.m., and I wondered if maybe the bar didn't open until the evening. I was about ready to have Bianca drive away and take a tour of the rest of the town when a dirty white sedan pulled in and parked right next to our van. Bianca turned the ignition off and threw me the keys.

"If we gotta make a run for it, you'll probably have to drive."

"You're the professional driver," I said. "You worked New York City, the craziest streets in the USA."

"You're right. I am the best. But if we're running out of here under fire, you'll have to drive because I'm going to be the one shooting."

"I don't see that turning out well for either of us."

Bianca shrugged. "Maybe let's just hope it doesn't come to that."

I tried to put the keys in my front pocket without success. The weight I'd put on the last few years due to my sedentary lifestyle and love of fast food had manifested itself mostly in my belly and my thighs, making even a regular set of keys rough to fit into my pocket. The monster rig that came with rental cars these days didn't stand a chance. I crammed it into my back pocket instead and wondered if anyone would notice if I stood the whole time instead of sitting down.

Bianca and I were the first to get out of our vehicle, and we both looked around paranoid, wondering if we were walking into an ambush or some other kind of trap. But then two tall white guys, one with a mustache and one with a shaved head, got out of the dirty sedan and Bianca cracked a smile. She ran to the shaved head guy and gave him a hug loaded with more warmth I suspected she was capable of.

"This is Teddy," she said, waving me over. "He was my dad's partner."

When she mentioned her dad, the warmth dissipated and the two of them separated, and Bianca wiped her eye with her fist. Teddy stepped toward me and held his hand out.

"Theo Abbott," he said. "This one's the only one who can get away with calling me Teddy anymore."

I shook his hand and looked at Bianca, who was still shivering and looking off blankly toward the bar. Something didn't sit right with me about that, but the whole thing was such a mess anyway that I'd learned to squash most of those warning signs. Not that warning signs mattered anyway. We all knew it was going to go to shit. The question was when it would happen and who would survive.

"And that sullen-looking son of a bitch over there is Inspector Greg Herren," Abbott said. "He's with Corrections."

"Corrections?" I asked. "I didn't know anyone from Corrections would be involved. What if Jay finds out?"

"Settle down, kid. He's been working with us for a while on this because of an identity theft scam running out of some of the facilities your family controls. It's got nothing to do with your family and looked like a perfect way for us to work together without raising suspicions. He just got a fancy certificate from the governor on account of how honest and forthright he is."

I know that was supposed to make me feel better about the whole thing, but it seemed like a case of protesting too much. Didn't matter though—this was who we had and at least working with someone from the department would raise our miniscule chance of success a bit.

"Doesn't look like anybody's here," Bianca said. "We just gonna talk out here in the parking lot like assholes?"

Theo smiled and produced a key ring from his back pocket.

"I know somebody who knows somebody," he said, then he looked over at Bianca. "You were here with your dad a few times early on when you were little. Probably don't remember much though."

She shook her head and stuck her fingers in her ears and dug around.

"Something about this this town feels familiar," she said. "But I don't remember any specifics. And I can't really concentrate on anything with that goddamn buzzing in my head."

"That's the windmills," Abbott said. "Folks who paid for 'em and make money off of 'em say the buzzing is just in people's heads, but folks in town beg to differ."

I rubbed my ears too and tried to knock the sound out. My ears always seemed to be buzzing though, so I never thought much about it until he said something. Now that was all I could think about.

"Seriously, can we get inside," Bianca said, looking around. I was a bit surprised how paranoid she was being, especially considering how close she was to one of the guys, and wondered if I should be more paranoid about what was going on.

We followed Theo around to the back of the bar where he opened the door and let us in. The place was dank, but not completely dark. There were a few lights burning and even though there were no windows, enough of the sunlight found its way in through cracks and crevices to give the place a hazy glow that made it easier to navigate the room without running into anything.

When someone eventually turned on all the lights, the place didn't look any better. It was a dive bar in the truest sense of the word. A bar off to one side with shitty bottles of shitty booze scattered across a mirrored shelf at the back commanded the bulk of the main room's attention. Rickety black leather stools bolted to the floor gave space for up to ten patrons to sit and drink their shitty booze without having to face another person except the bartender or whatever people were on the two giant, but outdated, televisions hanging on the wall.

Inspector Herren was the first person to take a seat. He pulled out a chair closest to the wall at a table near the back, in front of a video golf machine. The rest of us followed suit, filling in the seats at the table and dragging over a couple of chairs from a neighboring table. I ended up in the most awkward seat with my back to the bar and to the door and the jumbo ring of rental keys digging into my butt. Herren was also the first to talk, his voice surprisingly gruff.

"Tell us everything. It's all safe here."

I nodded and gave him a rundown of everything that had happened so far. It started with drips and drabs from what had happened with Posey and her brother and her stepbrothers and then, in a roundabout way, got around to Dutchy and the money, then Bianca's dad on the top of the parking garage in Brooklyn, and I just kept going. I told everything—strangling Dutchy included. I looked around the table when I was done, expecting glances of abject horror or judgment, but I just saw professional looking faces not at all shocked by the violence in my life. Bianca took my hand under the table and squeezed it. Could there be a chance that this would all work out right in the end?

"So you don't know the identity of the next victim on your list?" Abbott asked.

I was taken aback when he said *next* victim, like all of the others had been planned, but I don't think he meant anything by it and I certainly had no moral standing to be deriding him for it. So I just shook my head.

"I guess we're supposed to learn more when we get to the casino."

"And you're okay with being recorded?"

I nodded again. Couldn't quite bring myself to say yes out loud just yet.

"We really need to know that you're committed,"

125

Abbott said. "I don't want to put our asses out like this and then have you—"

"You just heard me lay my story out for you. That wasn't easy. *This* isn't easy. Trusting you. Trusting all of this. My entire life is a mess because of people like you fucking it all up. Sure, I haven't done much to make any of it better, but good goddammit when I say that I'm willing to do whatever needs to be done to take these assholes down, you can be sure I fucking mean it."

This time, the look on Abbott's face was the sort of shock and confusion I'd been expecting before. Herren remained stoic and Bianca cracked into a guttural laugh that eventually swept me into its goofy orbit. Abbott went behind the bar and drew four shots of something brown and four draft beers then brought them back to the table. Three of us clinked our glasses together in solidarity and dropped the shots into the beers and drank it all down. Herren didn't partake, and that's when I knew he was going to screw us over eventually.

Chapter Sixteen

Inspector Herren went back out to the car and Theo Abbott stayed behind for another round of shots.

"I don't like him," I said. "He seems judgy."

"He investigates other cops and tries to maintain some dignity and honor in his job. That's enough for me."

"During those shots though, he gave me a look that set me wrong. He's got something up his sleeve," I said.

"You're going to kill a man and he's going to be watching. That's bound to make a man nervous, I would imagine."

"He's not going to actually kill him," Bianca said, then she turned to me. "Right? I mean—"

"I was actually hoping to work that out with you guys," I said, trying to avoid eye contact with Bianca. "I mean, I'm not a cop...you heard my story. People die when I'm around and sometimes I'm the one pulling the trigger."

Abbott sighed and leaned back in his chair dramatically.

"You seem like an okay kid, despite all the murders and such, so I can tell you what's what. Right?"

I nodded.

"I'm long past naïve," I said.

Abbott rubbed his hands together and ran his fingers through his hair before leaning forward toward me.

"Officially," he said, "we don't want any casualties. We want a clean takedown and let these guys run the course of our fine justice system."

"And unofficially?" Bianca asked.

He leaned in even closer this time, and I thought he was going to jump across the table and grab me.

"The more of these slimy fuckers you can take out before it's over, the happier we'll all be."

This time it was Bianca's turn to have the look of abject horror. It seemed to just now be dawning on her that this was likely to be messy.

"I'm...I mean, we...this isn't what we had in mind. Dominick?"

"Come on, B," Theo said. "This can't be the first time it's occurred to you that there might be—"

Bianca interrupted him with another deep, throaty laugh that frightened me a bit. "Oh my god, the look on your face right now is priceless. The level of condescension between the two of you is enough to dry me up for men eternally."

Abbott cracked a smarmy smile, but I wasn't as easily convinced. She might be trying to throw us off, but there was enough emotion in that speech that I knew some of it was true. It was bad enough trying to work something like this out with rational professionals, but the amount of emotion swamping this adventure was damn near lethal. I knew it was all going to go south eventually, but I was still hoping if I died that it would be clean and quick. The more emotional baggage we were working with, the more of a chance there was for any of us to end up tied to a chair in a dark room waiting for a man with a bag of tools to carve us up slowly.

"Listen," Bianca said, "I don't do this serious shit. And listening to you try and work this out like some kind of hardcore gun crew is just too much. I think we all know the less we try and plan this out, the better off we'll all be. I'm not Miss Naivete either, guys, let's not make me scare the hell out of you two with my own confessional soliloquy."

We all stared at each other awkwardly for a beat or two and I half expected Abbott to go back behind the bar for another round of shots. But the awkward stare down was finally broken with the return of Inspector Herren.

"I played the phones a bit to see what I could get a line on, and it's dead out there. Nobody's talking."

"So maybe it's off?" Abbott asked.

"I think Jay's working this one outside of his regular system," I said. "He probably expects me to do something like this, and I'm not sure it really matters to him."

"Then what the hell are we all doing here?" Abbott asked.

I was finally starting to get my mind wrapped around where all of this was going and how to move forward without setting unrealistic expectations for everyone involved.

"Like the lady said, less planning, more observing. Get your men set up where they can see us and hear us, and I guarantee you before this is all over, you'll have enough on record to bring the entire family down."

"The entire family?" Herren asked.

"Yes, that includes me," I said. "If I survive."

Bianca took my hand again and rubbed the outside of

it with her thumb.

"These assholes have been all over my dad forever," she said. "They made his life hell and they may as well have been the ones to put the gun to his head in that parking garage."

She held our interconnected hands high over the table triumphantly.

"Considering what Dom and I have done together since we met, saying I'm part of the family seems creepy, but I think y'all get the idea. I'm all in if he's all in."

Abbott and I both blushed, but, again, Herren was the face of bland stability. He was jotting things down in a small black notebook with what looked like a fountain pen. I was impressed and wondered if my initial thought of his screwing us over was wrong. How bad could a guy with that kind of appreciation for writing utensils really be?

"Is that a fountain pen?" I asked, jumping out of my chair and wiggling my way through the others at the table to look over his shoulder.

"Uh, yeah. Makes me feel like writing is something special. Also, I tend to remember more when I use a pen like this."

"But what if someone walks away with it? Aren't those things like a hundred dollars or more?"

Herren held the pen up to me and waved it around, though he didn't look up from his notebook. "I...uh, this was about fifteen bucks, I think. My wife got it for me. I'd never pay a hundred dollars for a pen. Well, maybe one of those space pens that writes upside down and under water."

"Can I try it? I don't remember if I mentioned it or not—or if anyone told you—but I'm a writer. A novelist, actually. Published novelist, and I'm always looking for new things to add to my process."

I thought this would bond us together with an oath of inky creativity, but it seemed to turn him even further away from me. He snapped the pen away from my face and slid it and the notebook into his front pocket.

"Take your time getting to the hotel and we'll work on getting a team set up in the probable areas for your mission. We'll be in touch when we're ready."

"What was the brand of that pen?" I asked, trying once more to make our bond happen. "When this is all done I want to get back to—"

He stood with his back to me and turned to face Bianca.

"Agent Abbott will be your primary contact from this point forward," he said. "If you hear from me again, it will be because things have gone horribly awry."

And with that, he was gone, and I was back to assuming he would be the source of this plan's downfall.

"What in the hell was that?" I asked the table after he was gone.

"Greg is…intense. It's one of the reasons he's so good at what he does and why he's one of the few people who doesn't mind calling out bad apples, even if they're part of his own unit."

"I don't get honest from him. I get creepy."

"Well," Abbott said slowly, "in another version of this plan, you're exactly the kind of guy he would be looking to take down."

"Like I said before. He's judgy and I think that's going to come back and bite us in the ass."

Bianca was the one to go for shots this time, but instead of bringing back a round for the table, she stayed behind the bar and drank directly from a bottle of rum.

"Enough of the character evaluations," she said. "The less we think about the motives and emotional maturity of those involved, the better we'll all be."

"She's right," Abbott said. "Let's talk specifics about the surveillance we'll be providing."

"Wouldn't it be better if we didn't know?" I asked. "You know, plausible deniability and such."

"I'm not sure how that would work."

"I'm just afraid that if we know too much, we'll be hyper aware of it and keep looking at the camera and stuff. I took a video production class once and the people who weren't aware of the camera always looked so much more natural than the ones who knew where the cameras were."

"We're not on a reality show, Dominick," Bianca said. "Is this what Parker meant when he talked about you always trying to frame your life as a movie?"

"Parker? Are you two best friends now? Did he like the goodies you showed him in that dinner dress? Is that why you're here with me?"

Even as I could feel the ridiculous emotion building inside of me and knew I was about to spew a fountain of garbage, I was amazed at how well Bianca was taking my paranoid ramblings. We did seem to be a good fit for each other and maybe if things didn't go to complete shit after this thing, there was a future we could pursue together.

And then I said, "Did Jay set this up? Did he send an advance team to scout you for his time? Make up that whole story about you father and—"

She was across the bar and in front of my face swinging a peeling knife faster than was humanly possible and laid me out with a smack to the face so hard it echoed in my nose.

"If you ever talk about my father like that again, I'll ram this knife down your throat and cut your stomach out. Do you understand?"

I wanted to nod, but the peeling knife was so close to my throat that a hard swallow could kill me, so I tried to convey my agreement with my eyes. She finally stepped away from me and went back behind the bar.

"Tell us everything," she said to Abbott.

Chapter Seventeen

When we got back on the road, I had to drive because Bianca had worked her way through an entire bottle of rum while Theo Abbott clued us in on his big master plan. Master plan might have been too elaborate a definition though because, even after talking about it for an hour, it amounted to little more than: Abbott had people everywhere and they'd be able to record whatever we did, good or bad. Anytime I tried to get more specifics, I was shot down or made to look like a fool, so I stopped trying. If his plan didn't end up working, he would be on the worse end of it than I would be. Probably.

Bianca slept the rest of the way to the casino. I left her in the van with it running when we arrived so she could sleep off the rest of whatever was bothering her while I got us checked in. Compared to the luxurious lobby and gilded extremes of the MGM Grand in Detroit, the Pleasantwood Casino and Resort lobby was rustic and understated. A giant fireplace was the focus of the entire area and check-in was a small square of desks off to the side. I was the only one there to check in, and three staff members waited to help me.

We all made small talk as the clerk sitting closest to

me worked a computer checking for my reservation. One of the clerks, a tall woman with long hair below her waist, complimented me on the minivan. I was taken aback by that because even though the parking lot was thinly populated, I hadn't parked very close to the hotel and there was no way she could have seen me get out of the van from where she was standing. I wondered if this was a passive-aggressive way of Abbott and his crew letting me know that what he said about always watching me was true.

As the small talk grew annoying and the topics stretched further away from my comfort zone, the clerk at the computer had a confused look on his face.

"Can you spell the name on the reservation again?"

"I wasn't the one who made the actual reservation. I wonder if it might have accidentally been put under Jay Taylor."

More clicking at the keyboard, then: "Ah, okay. So it does seem that's the name under the reservation, but your room is over at the water park."

No.

"I think that's a mistake. I'm here for an event at the casino, and he said my room was at the casino. The water park is *not* the casino."

"I'm sorry, sir, but the reservation explicitly requests the water park. It's certainly part of the casino property and we consider you part of our resort family. There's even—"

"When was that reservation made?"

"Um, it looks like Mr. Taylor made the reservation about a month ago."

So he'd made it even before he knew I'd be the one showing up and going through with this. Then why not mention the water park? Was that a piece of the puzzle I was supposed to figure out? I thought initially it might have been a subtle hint that Jay knew we rented a minivan and suspected what we were up to.

"That doesn't make any sense," I said. "I hate water parks."

"It looks like Mr. Taylor reconfirmed the reservation just a few minutes ago as well."

Wait a minute.

"When he confirmed it, is that when it was switched to the water park?"

"I can't see that level of detail in this reservation note. I can get a manager and—"

"No, that's okay. Thanks. How do I get to the water park?"

He gave me a map and let me know a shuttle ran every fifteen minutes between the casino and the water park. I stomped back out to the van and screamed at Bianca when I opened the door.

"GoddammotherfuckingJay," I said. Twice. "He's onto us. We're so fucked."

Bianca was still in that groggy state you get when you wake up from a car nap too quickly and your muscles hurt and you have no idea where you are or why there's so much drool on your face. But I kept ranting.

"What are we supposed to do at a water park?" Bianca asked, still not quite getting the full impact of what the change meant.

"I don't know, but it's not good. He knows we rented the minivan, so he probably knows we met with Abbott and Herren. He's onto us."

She wriggled in her seat a few times and stretched, then it looked like she had more clarity in her eyes.

"So what?"

"Huh?'

"He's not a moron. You're not a moron. You figured he'd get wise to it anyway. He's taunting us. Trying to throw us off our game. Just do what we came here to do and don't let him get in your head."

"We're way past that. This whole family has a fucking base camp set up in my head."

She grabbed me by the shoulders and pulled me closer to her. "And that's what I'm here for," she said. "To keep your head on straight and provide…alternative distractions."

"Oh."

"He's not the first guy who's tried to screw you over, is he?"

"No."

"And how did it work out for the others who tried?"

I smiled thinking about their bodies. I didn't like how happy that made me.

"Still," I said. "Who wants to spend the weekend at a fucking water park?"

"Could be fun. Maybe it'll bring out my maternal instincts? We can steal one of the little shits and pretend we're a family."

Check-in at the water park was noisier and far more stressful. I don't know what it was doing to Bianca's maternal instincts and sex drive, but it was making me think a life of virtue and abstinence would not be at all bad right then. In addition to the echoing sound of screaming kids and the smell of chlorine everywhere, everything was slippery and wet. I popped a hip and almost split my pants trying to overcorrect on a fall and not hit my head on the floor. Bianca laughed at me and made no effort to help.

When we finally made our way through the thicket of families ahead of us, we either didn't look as suspiciously single and childless as I thought we did, or the clerk was so worn down and out of it that she didn't care. Either way, we were presented with an envelope that contained yellow wristbands for the water park, gift certificates for a free breakfast the next morning, and keys to what was referred to as the "family suite." I had no idea what that meant, but assumed we'd be walking into a room full of changing stations and garishly colored wallpaper.

We were both delightfully surprised though when we opened the double-doors to the suite and saw the same blandly offensive Native American décor that ran through the rest of the hotel spread across enough space for several families to set up house. It wasn't anything that would compete with the presidential suite at one of the Strip hotels in Vegas, but I wasn't a Hollywood leading man or rock star on tour either, so my expectations were minimal. Bianca seemed suitably impressed as well, especially as we made our way through the foyer and into the main living area that was floor-to-ceiling windows looking out over a wildlife preserve.

"I can barely hear the screaming kids," Bianca said.

I took a deep breath through my nose and waved my hands in the air. "And I don't smell a whiff of chlorine."

We both flopped down on the L-shaped couch facing the windows, and after admiring the view for a while, we looked at each other—obviously on the same page— and realized we didn't have any luggage.

"We should have brought our fancy clothes from

dinner at least," Bianca said.

"I do miss that sport coat, and I think it would have been cool to see how it looked with a gun crammed in the pocket."

"That's quite a come on line, sir."

"Ugh. I can't even think about that right now. My mental space is about as unerotic as possible, I think."

"Whatever. I can't imagine there's anything worth buying down in that guest shop. You think maybe the casino shops have some fancy duds?"

I hopped off the couch, wandered toward the master bedroom off to my left, and stood in front of the massive closet at the furthest end of the room. I don't know exactly how much longer it was before Bianca came up behind me and stared at it as well.

"I don't want to know," I said.

"It would certainly be creepy, if not incredibly convenient."

"And it's right in his wheelhouse of psychological warfare. But I just don't see how it's possible. I can understand him calling ahead and screwing with us that way, because he wouldn't have to leave his desk. And I guess he could have had someone from the hotel buy clothes for us and sneak them in here before we arrived."

"When you say it like that, it's not quite so implausible."

"But still creepy," I said.

"Creepy as fuck."

I had my hand on the door, ready to open it, when there was a loud knock from the foyer. Bianca and I both looked up the ceiling, instinctively wondering about cameras. I briefly forgot how paranoid and freaked out I was by the whole thing as I noticed that was the third time in a short period that she and I had been in sync on our motions. Maybe I'd bring that up later and see what kind of discussion came of it. Probably nowhere near any of the kids around though, her allegedly off-handed comment about her maternal instincts still had me freaked out. All that panic went out the door though, replaced by fresh, new panic when Bianca opened the door and let Parker Farmington into the suite. He had two garment bags slung over his arms and pulled a large black rolling suitcase behind him. The fitted black suit with white shirt and no tie made him look more fashionable and formidable than I'd ever seen him in my life.

"No," I said, louder than I wanted. "Get out."

I waved my finger at him in an accusatory manner and felt weird about it, but I just wanted him away from me even if that made me feel like an old fortune teller woman spitting at the feet of someone threatening to curse their children.

"Darling," Bianca said, sounding like a parody of a Tennessee Williams character, "we have a guest and you'll be polite."

"I don't like this. He's a bad omen. This whole thing is—"

"*I'm* a bad omen?" Parker asked. "I think someone needs to look in his own cursed mirror."

"That doesn't even make any sense," I screamed.

I shook my hands out and waved my arms around, trying to expel the rage and paranoia that was working its way through my system, but I could feel it taking over. Even as I knew this was exactly what Jay wanted, I let myself be absorbed by its comforting hate and violence. Parker was saying something to Bianca about what a goober I was, so I ran at him as fast as I could, with my head pulled down, and blasted him square in the chest.

We both went flying over the corner of the couch and I thought Bianca screamed, but it was actually Parker. I tried to punch him twice, but he dodged them easily and kneed me in the groin instead. After rolling into a ball to buy myself some time, Bianca grabbed Parker from behind.

I thought she was going to be neutral and try to break the fight up, but she wrapped one of her arms around his neck and said, "Remember where I pulled that money from I gave you last time?"

He nodded, as best as he could in a headlock, and I came out of my ball and stood up. She yanked her arm up more, snapped his head back, and shoved him down so she could look into his eyes.

"I kept a knife there too."

I smiled as she taunted him, feeling cocky in her protective orbit. But I should have known to never count Parker Farmington out. Bianca spun him out of her grip and threw him to the ground. She tugged out some knots in her hair and was going to put her foot on Parker's head when I saw him reaching for something. I didn't think she was lying about her knife—and it wouldn't have even surprised me if she had a gun on her—but the thought of Parker carrying a weapon never even crossed my mind. I was stunted in action trying to process that thought.

Parker was quick on the draw though. He pulled something small and black from inside his suit jacket and pressed it to Bianca's thigh. I waited for the sound of a gunshot, but instead saw Bianca spasm, stick her tongue out of her mouth, then fall to the ground. As quickly as he pulled what I assume was a stun gun from his coat, Parker turned and came after me. I grabbed the biggest vase I could find from the table by the door to the suite and threw it at him, slowing his approach, but not stopping it.

"What the hell, Parker? Who gave you a fucking Taser?"

"I told you I was here to make sure you didn't screw this up. But here you are...screwing it up."

He was wobbling back and forth, waving the Taser in my direction, but not making any progress toward me that I was worried about.

"Are you working with Jay, or is this some weird freelance thing you've got going on?"

This time I expected him to make a run at me, and I clenched my muscles in anticipation, but he started crying instead.

"Always with the bullshit. You can't just take a hint and move on. You always have to find a way to...I don't know. Look at me. Even I can't come up with the right words to describe how awful you've become."

Even though I'd the same thoughts about myself, I was offended to hear them from Parker. We'd had a bit of a breakthrough after our first mess together and I thought we were moving in the right direction. But this side of him was new.

I grabbed another vase, just in case he came at me again, but kept it in a defensive position. I also noticed Bianca was starting to move again and recover from her Taser blast. I needed to keep Parker talking until she was back to full(ish) strength.

"Put the Taser down and let's talk this out. We've got history, man. It shouldn't come to—"

He rushed me again, and even though I dodged his outstretched Taser, I was still amazed by how quickly he was moving for an overweight, middle-aged, destitute former writing professor. Could he be juicing? Why? Better writing speed? Would that work for me?

Our weird little dance moved around the outer edge of the living area toward the giant windows, and along the way I swapped the vase for a fireplace poker. Bianca was still stirring but hadn't made any movements toward standing up. I swung the poker lazily every once in a while to keep Parker on guard, and he did the same with the Taser.

"We never talked about her last words," Parker said, moving in a little closer.

"Posey's? I try not to think about it."

When I mentioned Posey's name, he snarled and took two steps closer to me. I knew he'd been having a relationship with Posey when we first met, but I didn't think it would still affect him like this.

"Not Posey, jackass. Lindsey. You were in the car with her before she died...I just want to know what she said."

I gripped the poker with two hands and moved my feet into a defensive stance. This wasn't going to stay quiet and pathetic for long, and I wanted to be ready for his charge this time.

"She saved me, we talked about that. You said—"

The snarling was back in his voice. I knew he and Lindsey had developed some kind of weird mutual crush that led to a more stable and formalized relationship, but the last time Parker and I had interacted, he seemed at peace with her death and my role in it. I was very curious what—or who—had changed his mind about that.

143

"You said you would make her death worth it and you lied. You're a curse."

"As many times as I've heard that, I keep expecting it to hurt less, but—"

He stepped toward me with the Taser outstretched and instead of worrying about dodging his increasingly more stable and valiant attacks, I was wondering why he was using a Taser instead of a gun. With the crowd he was traveling in these days, it seemed like a gun would be easier to come by than a fucking Taser. So he had it for a reason. Either he didn't want to kill me, just send me a message, or he didn't want to kill me quickly. I'd known Parker half a decade by that point in our relationship, and while he was always petty and vindictive, he never struck me as the slow-burning tortuous type either. He was, like me, more prone to passionate outbursts than decades-long revenge planning.

Which meant he probably talked to some people who put it in his head that I was responsible for his true love's death, and he came her to tase me in the nuts or whatever to make it right. End of story. And honestly, I probably deserved it. So I eased my defensive stance and was about to drop my poker as Parker dove toward me once more when he gasped and grunted, then fell to the ground. Bianca was standing in front of me with a bloody knife in her hand and a look of abject horror on her face at what she had just done.

Chapter Eighteen

"Oh fuck," I said. "What did you do? What the…"

"I was saving you," Bianca said, still holding the knife she had stabbed Parker with.

"Oh Jesus," I said. "Fuck fuck fuck."

I looked down at Parker, who wasn't moving, but I sure as hell wasn't going to lean down and check for a pulse. My worst fear right then was that he would still be alive and I'd have to make an impossible decision. But the fact I even considered not taking him to a hospital if he was still alive said more about me than I was comfortable thinking about. I knew I was bad. I knew I was despicable and certainly borderline sociopathic. But was I also evil?

"What do we do? Is he dead. Is he—"

"He's dead," I said. "End of story. No more questions."

"Then what do we do with him?"

"I don't know. Jesus. Why did you stab him?"

"He shot me with a fucking Taser," she said, waving the knife at me now. "And he was about to do the same to you."

"So what? It's a Taser, not a shotgun. Or a fucking knife."

Bianca was still holding the knife as she danced around in front of me in her panicked state. I wanted her to put it down because I was afraid she'd decide I was berating her too much and come after me too. So I toned down my rhetoric, even as I continued to panic on the inside. She must have sensed a change in my demeanor after that because she slowed her dance to more of a pacing, and she wiped the knife off on her pants and set it down on the coffee table next to where Parker was lying. I thought I saw him move, but I convinced myself that it was just my mind playing tricks on me and the adrenaline doing wonky things to my vision.

"Should we call someone?"

"Like the cops? No way. I don't want to—"

"Like Jay, maybe."

"Again with Jay," I said. "You want Jay to help us, you want to go to a gun range at Jay's house. No, we're not going to call Jay. We have a limited opportunity here to do something right and the only way this plan works is if Jay has faith that we'll go through with it."

"I think he might still be—"

"No. Don't say it. There is no good that can come from finishing that thought."

"Easy for you to say since you aren't the one who stabbed him."

"Then you shouldn't have fucking stabbed him. Jesus. My head is killing me and we need to sort this house."

"So again I ask, should we—"

"No we're not going to call anybody. I know this suite doesn't take up the entire floor, but you've got to imagine the walls are soundproofed or something like that. For parties and whatnot?"

She shrugged. "I don't know Dominick. I don't get myself into these messes as much as you do."

"Really? You think *now* is the time to start being judgmental of me? When you're using my fucked-up life and bad luck to get revenge on the people who killed your dad?"

"I'm not trying to call your shit, Dom. I'm just saying this isn't my jam. This isn't what I do, so I'm not real good at fixing the shit when it falls apart."

"If you haven't noticed," I said, "neither am I."

She shrugged again and took her shirt and pants off.

"Fine," she said. "We'll improvise then."

I wasn't sure if she really was that messed up sexually that this turned her on, or if she'd seen too many romantic suspense stories that used sex as much for plots points as action movies used car chases and gun fights. But the only part of me it was arousing was my anger.

"Stop with the lame attempts at seduction. Our lives are on the line here and we can't be stopping every hour for a quickie."

She looked down at the pile of clothes in front of her, then at Parker's slumped body, then finally at the bloody knife.

"I'm not going to get offended that seeing me like this doesn't arouse you. I'm just going to point out that I'm not some nymphomaniac action junkie looking to get her rocks off in a tense situation."

"I'm sorry. I shouldn't have—"

"I'm just a girl, who just stabbed a guy, and I don't want to wear the bloody clothes any longer than I have to."

"Oh. Right. God, I'm a moron. And probably a

pervert, it seems."

"No arguments here from me."

"So what we do is get out of here for a bit. Clear our heads, clear the air, and—"

"Dump the body?"

"No. Leave him. And leave your clothes. There are cameras all over the place out there and I don't want to risk being on camera getting rid of bloody clothes."

"What about housekeeping?"

"We'll put the Do Not Disturb sign up."

"And if they ignore it?"

"We can't cover every base, but I'm more secure knowing that when Jay booked this room, he made it very clear that nobody was to come up here because he wants to control the situation. So it's not a perfect solution, but it's the best we have. And we're not going to be gone long."

"Shouldn't we at least roll him in a blanket and shove him in the closet or something, just in case some nosey maid stumbles in here by accident?"

"Fine. Good point. See, you're better at this than you let on."

"That's not something I want to be proud of," she said, squatting down next to Parker. "Go find a big blanket and I'll make sure he's not wearing a wire or anything."

Oh shit. That was not even something I had ever considered. What if Parker was working for the cops too? Oh shit. Shit shit *shit.*

"Shit," I said. "But if he was working with the cops or something, wouldn't they have busted down the door by now?"

"Maybe they don't know he's dead yet?"

"Shit. We could walk out there and be swarmed by cops once they realize what happened."

"I was just joking, dude. I don't think he was working with the cops."

"The minute I saw him I knew something was messed up. He was never going to let me go down easy."

"Look at your life, man. Fate was never going to let you go down easy."

I left her to search the body while I searched the suite for a blanket big enough to wrap a body in. There were two of them in the main bedroom, and I brought both of them out.

"If it makes you feel any better, I'm pretty sure he's dead," she said.

"Long-term, no. That doesn't make me feel any better. But right here, right now, it does make things easier."

We wrapped him up in both blankets, crammed him into the largest of the closets, and made sure the door closed tightly. Bianca threw her bloody clothes into one of the plastic bags hanging in the bathroom that was supposed to be for wet swimsuits and hid it in the rolling suitcase still sitting by the door. The only clothes for her in the suitcase were a swimsuit and pullover or several dresses, so she changed into a pair of dress pants and a white shirt identical to what Parker had been wearing that I assumed had been meant for me. She looked a whole lot better in it than I would have. As I was washing the knife by hand for the second time before trying to run it through the dishwasher, I heard her squeal. When I looked over to her, she was holding a small handgun like one of the ones we'd shot with at Jay's gun range.

"Well isn't this interesting," she said.

"Could be one of Jay's, could be his own."

"Could be a plant, too. So why the Taser if he had this on him?"

"Maybe he didn't know it was in there."

"Maybe someone sent him in here with a gun to take care of business and he thought he could do you a solid by not killing you and just zapping you instead."

"Sure would be easier to clear all of this up if someone hadn't stabbed him to death."

"Someone wouldn't have had to stab him to death if someone else wouldn't have antagonized him and bum rushed him when he came through the door."

"Just put the gun away and let's get out of here."

Bianca tucked the gun into the back of her dress pants and untucked the shirt to hide it. On me, the outfit would have looked disheveled and lame. On her it looked disheveled and dangerous.

We walked along the outer edge of the water park property and I could feel the stress of everything easing with each step in the sunshine. I was wearing jeans, which were probably too warm for the weather, but I'd spent so much time in air-conditioned buildings and automobiles that I'd forgotten it was the dead of summer. But even with the swampy warmth that comes with wearing jeans in summer, it felt good to be outside. Bianca must have been feeling the same thing because she rolled up the sleeves on her dress shirt and unbuttoned the shirt down enough to be borderline scandalous.

"I wish I could kick my shoes off and run through the grass barefoot," I said.

She smiled and grabbed my hand. "Do it. I'll do it too."

She didn't wait for me to follow before using her right foot to flick off her left shoe and then pulling off her other shoe and her socks and tossing them off the sidewalk path. My sneakers had laces and were harder to get off without fully stopping and I almost fell once while doing it, but soon enough I was frolicking through the grass behind Bianca. When I got close enough, she grabbed my hand again and pulled me toward the fountain at the center of the field.

I thought it was odd that there was a fountain in the middle of a field, but much of the layout of the water park didn't make sense to me. I'm sure there was a reason for it all, but I also realized I was not the ideal customer for a water park. As we frolicked around, I noticed that on the other side of the fountain was a drop-off and a massive hill that led to an open air theater that linked the water park grounds with the casino grounds. Part of me wondered then if that was part of the plan to begin with. But then I remembered the clerk telling me that Jay had updated the reservation right before we arrived. There was no way to tell if the confirmation had involved switching the reservation from the casino to the water park though, so maybe the plan had always been to put us up at the water park.

"Are you thinking what I'm thinking?" I asked.

"Hell yeah," she said. "That sounds a lot like New Kids on the Block down there."

"No, I mean, look at how this area connects to the casino. I wonder if that's why we were booked here."

"I thought you said the reservation was changed before we got here."

"I know, but he couldn't confirm the change involved switching properties. Maybe it was to upgrade us. Or maybe it was just to check to make sure they hadn't given the reservation away."

"So you overreacted like a bonehead is what you're saying?"

"I'm not even going to justify that with a response considering your little adventure in overreaction."

"I've wanted to see New Kids on the Block since I was a kid. My mom and I were supposed to go the night she died."

"Damn," I said. "That's awful. Don't you have bad memories from that?"

"No way. It was our big thing together. We'd been trying to go forever, but that was at peak New Kids and, well, with a dad on a cop's salary and a mom working in an office, we had to get the cheap seats and they were always the first to sell out."

"That looks like a pretty big crowd," I said. "What if this one is sold out too?"

She winked at me and pulled me down the hill toward the theater. "I've learned a *lot* about sneaking in places since then."

"I don't know, we've got a schedule to keep and there's the matter of—"

"I know what's in our room, Dominick. I don't have amnesia. But if this is all going to go to shit while we're here, how about giving a girl one last shot to see her childhood heartthrobs before she dies or gets sent to prison?"

"Whatever. You go listen to the boy band and I'll do some scouting to see if there's an obvious advantage for us to be booked here."

"No way, buddy. You're my plus one. You can't leave a gal alone at a concert like that. What if someone takes advantage of me?"

"You left your knife back in the room, so I'm sure they'll be fine."

"Aren't you funny. Come on."

I was right about the show being sold out. As we got closer to the theater, I saw waves and waves of people filling every seat plus most of the surrounding space and out into a grassy area. They all seemed to be female and around my age.

"Looks like the Venn diagram of casino customers and water park customers has a pretty solid New Kids on the Block center," I said.

"Moms with too much stress and too much money. Both of those hotels are probably full of exhausted dads taking care of the kids while mom and her drunk friends from book club or wine club or whatever fawn all over their teenage crushes."

As she said that, something tickled the back of my mind. More and more it seemed like our location was not payback for renting the minivan and meeting with the cops but rather part of the original plan. Was the guy I was supposed to kill one of those beleaguered dads up in the hotel watching his kids while his wife was at the concert? If so, why hadn't Jay told me? If it was supposed to happen during the concert, we should have been told by now, right? Oh. Crap.

And once again, Bianca seemed to be on the same page mentally as me.

"This is when it's supposed to happen, isn't it?" she said.

"What if Parker was bringing us our instructions and gear for tonight?"

"I don't know. The clothes in the suitcase looked too

formal for an outdoor concert. And why would you have formal clothes if you're supposed to take out one of the dads?"

"He never actually mentioned the gender of our target. What if it's somebody *at* the concert? A woman."

"Then the clothes make even less sense."

Lightbulb.

"Shit. The suite. The formal clothes. What if we have VIP access to the concert? That seems more like the kind of person Jay would have business with, not some blue-collar momma in jeans and a bedazzled 'I Love Joey' T-shirt."

Bianca lightbulb.

"I bet there's a limo waiting for us. Let's go."

Chapter Nineteen

Bianca grabbed my hand again and dragged me all the way up the hill, never even stopping to pick up our shoes. When we got back into the room, we checked first to make sure Parker was still where he was supposed to be, then I sent Bianca into the main bathroom to get ready while I called the front desk to see what I could find out about a possible limo ride. It only took two tries to get ahold of someone who could confirm that a car reservation had been made under my name and that it was waiting downstairs right then as we spoke.

"They think we're rich," Bianca said, as I encouraged her to hurry the hell up and get ready. "If we're too eager they'll think something is up."

"I'm sure they run into rich people every once in a while who are polite and timely."

"Not who are our age and not at a place like this. You think our friend in the closet will be fine this much longer?"

"I've been involved several times at the state where the person dies, but body disposal has never been anything I've ever stuck around for other than the one time in

155

Ohio, but that was…let's not talk about that. Just hurry, please."

I went back out to the living area and stared off into the nature preserve, hoping to tap into some of its soothing vibes. As I looked out though, everything seemed almost too perfect. So much so that I actually had to walk right up to the glass and touch it to make sure it wasn't a high definition video screen showing us beautiful nature like in *Back to the Future Part II*. But it was real. So real, in fact, that as I was gazing further into the heart of the preserve, I saw Theo Abbott and a man I didn't recognize working their weight along the edge of the preserve toward the fountain and, I assumed, the theater below.

"Hey, B, come out here and look at this for a second."

"I said I'll be ready when I'm damn ready. This is important to me."

"No, I'm not hurrying you again. This is just…you've got to see this."

She waited a few more minutes before she finally joined me at the window. By this time Abbott and his friend were moving along a path that made me even more confident they were headed toward the theater and the concert.

"Sonofabitch," she said. "Who's that with him?"

"I was hoping you'd recognize him. I got nothing."

"This doesn't change anything though, does it? I mean we go to the site, do the job, and let them do their jobs."

"I guess, yeah. I mean they said they'd always be watching, so even though we didn't put it together right away what was going on, because someone killed the messenger—"

"Stop bringing that up, seriously. It's killing morale around here."

"He said they were always watching. That they'd know what was going on without us needing to be wired or to tell them," I said.

"You already said that part, and it's obvious it was true because there they are."

"Does that mean they know about Parker?"

Beat.

"Uh," she said, eloquently.

"We wondered about Jay and his folks knowing, but it never occurred to me about the cops watching."

"We did talk about him working with the cops and them busting down the door if they thought we killed one of their guys."

"But he was working for Jay, bringing us our gear for tonight. So they know, but they're not invested in busting down the door to avenge him or anything."

"You're starting to lose me. What should we do?"

"Keep pushing forward. Stay on task. Finish getting ready and we'll go meet the car."

"And you think Parker will stay fresh the rest of the night?"

"It's air conditioned, right? I'm sure he'll be fine. And with the smell of chlorine and rotten kids stinking up this place, I'm sure it would be a while before they even noticed his rotting smell anyway."

The car waiting for us was an SUV, not a limousine, and I had uncomfortable flashbacks to the last time Bianca and I were on an SUV with Parker driving us.

"I'm sure this is a coincidence," Bianca said.

"I'm sure you want to believe it is," I said.

I was tempted to sit in the front to try and establish some sort of dominance, but that seemed silly upon second thought and as Bianca had mentioned earlier, we were supposed to be rich people in the presidential suite and people like that sat in the back seat.

We were silent on the drive over to the casino, which I was sure to the driver came off as hoity-toity elegance, but was really just Bianca and I panicking inside of our heads and trying not to scream about how awful everything was turning out. The only thought I had related to my wealthy status at all was whether or not I had any cash in my wallet to tip the driver when he dropped us off. But then I wondered if rich people were even expected to tip. Did reach people carry cash? Wouldn't the assistant or whoever handled the reservations for the car have added the tip? By the time my mind swung back around to realize how ridiculous the entire train of thought was, we'd arrived at the casino's VIP entrance.

I opened my door but hesitated to get out, wondering if I was supposed to wait for the driver to open the door. Bianca remained firmly in place and seemed much more natural than I did in this world. Which seemed odd, honestly, for a girl raised by a cop and a secretary. But as I sat there with my hand on the half-opened door, she reached into a small purse I hadn't even noticed she was carrying and pulled out a single bill that she effortlessly traded with the driver for a small manila envelope, then opened her own door. I followed her in like a giddy kid following a magician after a birthday show asking how he did his tricks.

"What the hell was that?" I asked.

"What was what? The tip?"

"The effortless tip, the trade for the envelope? How do you know how to do all of this stuff?"

"When you grow up poor, well, what I considered poor, if you want the finer things in life, you have to act like you belong and learn the signals and the behaviors of the native tribes of the wealthy."

"Huh," I said. "That sounds shameless."

"Call it what you want, but it worked for us. Oh, crap."

"What?"

She was rifling through the collection of papers in the envelope, then pulled two tickets out of the mix and handed them over to me.

"We're not going to the concert," she said. "We're going to the murder mystery dinner here in the ballroom."

"That sounds just awful," I said. "Are you sure?"

"Look at the tickets."

This whole thing just kept getting better and better. I stared at the tickets then at the flyer for the event Bianca handed me, wondering if it was all part of some cosmic coincidence so large as to be astounding or if it was Jay digging into me even more.

"Booked for Death," I said, reading from the flyer. "An evening of book-themed murder and mayhem as Henning Price finds himself playing sleuth instead of author when his agent is murdered at the launch party for his first mystery novel."

"Sounds right up your alley," Bianca said. "Must be nice."

"This has to be Jay fucking with me. This is bullshit."

The last thing in the envelope was a black-and-white headshot of a pretentious-looking guy about my age wearing a turtleneck and thick black glasses. Bianca handed the photo to me and shook out the envelope to make sure there were no other surprises inside.

"Looks like our target is part of the show. Wonder if it's the author. That would be kind of hilarious."

"I don't get how some actor in a roadshow murder mystery got involved with Jay in a way that would result in his death. Jay's not a bookie or even really a traditional gangster. They all deal with cops and courts and criminals in the corrections system."

"Maybe it's payback. Like he has family involved with Jay or something."

"I guess, but it all still seems a bit too close to home for me, if you know what I mean."

"I think you're being paranoid and that's the worst thing you can be going into something like this. Just keep true and see how things develop. Did you bring the gun from the room?"

I nodded and tapped the back of my suit where I'd tucked it.

"I guess it makes sense that we're in the ballroom," I said, as we walked down the long main hallway following the signs. "The concert arena and the outdoor theater both have metal detectors. But the ballroom doesn't."

"Perfect then. Let's go enjoy the murder and mayhem."

"I can't help but wonder how much easier all of this would be if we had been able to get our full instructions from Parker before one of us—"

"Goddamit, Dominick, I told you not to bring that up again. And I also told you that if you hadn't gotten him all riled up—"

"I know, I know. I'm yelling at myself as much as I'm yelling at you."

"For a writer, you sure do suck at communication."

"I haven't been a writer in a long time," I said. "I've done more killing than writing lately. Maybe I should get new business cards made up."

We were outside of the ballroom now and I expected Bianca to take my hand as we entered, but she grabbed the tickets from me and pushed ahead to the greeter to be the first one in. As we thought would be the case with the concert, our stay in the presidential suite earned us VIP seating at the murder mystery dinner. This meant a table by ourselves right in the front of the room near the cluster of staging items where the murder mystery players were gathered as opposed to one of the larger community tables scattered through the rest of the ballroom. As much as I'd been involved in the mystery writing community and as much as I like reading them, I'd never been to a murder mystery dinner before and had no idea what to expect. I couldn't imagine Bianca had ever been to one either, but it also wouldn't surprise me if I found out she had been to one, had acted in one, and hell, had even written one.

"It's funny when you think about it," Bianca said as we took our seats. "That this whole mess got started with a mystery theater opportunity and here we are, near the end, at another mystery theater opportunity."

"You can in no way compare what should have been my New York City debut on the legitimate stage to this collection of…whatever they are."

"How long did you know Dutchy? Would you call anything he ever touched legitimate?"

Her mention of Dutchy flashed me back to that swampy trailer in the Bermuda Triangle of Brooklyn, looking down over Dutchy's dead body. That one hurt the most. I'd hated him so much for what I thought he was trying to do to me, but he'd been the first one of any of the people I knew from that part of my life who saw me as a writer.

Even if his whole aim was to screw me over, he knew enough about me to know that writing was my passion and the one thing I loved enough to draw me into his plan and keep me bamboozled long enough to use me to get his money. And had my wife's family not hounded me so hard and followed me to the city and pushed Bianca's dad to his end in my orbit, well he very well might still be alive and millions of dollars richer while I rotted away in one of those watery graves under an illegal trailer park in Brooklyn.

"Wait a minute," I said. "Weren't you the one who was supposed to be writing the script for the show?"

"Already wrote it. And it's good. If I thought I could compliment you on the story it's based on without things getting all weird between us, I would."

"Oh man, I'd heard rumors that was true but I thought Dutchy was just messing with me."

"Tis true," she said. "Shhhhh, now. It looks like things are about to start."

"If his entire plan was just to get me to stumble across the money before anyone could kill me, then why did he go to the effort of hiring out a script?"

"The money was only part of the plan. Dutchy loved that theater and loved theater. He really did want to make the show work and use it as his comeback vehicle."

Mixed with my resurfacing memories of his hasty wake, that news hit me even harder than it probably would have otherwise. So hard, in fact, that I started to cry. Once again I expected Bianca's comforting grip on my arm or leg, but since we'd arrived at the casino, she'd been cold to me. As the MC took the small stage at the front of the room, Bianca not only didn't comfort me, she scooted a few inches away from me.

As the MC babbled on, I was trolling memory lane with my high school self, reliving the best of Dutchy, and I didn't even realize the game was afoot until the lights went out and I heard a pop that sounded like a firecracker. The lights stayed out after that long enough that people in the crowd began stirring and wondering out loud if something was wrong.

I knew for a fact something was wrong when I heard a thump and a crash close to me, then the lights came on with Parker's wrapped-up body on the table in front of me and Cristal Hate smiling a crooked smile and pointing a gun at my face.

Chapter Twenty

While I stared at the gun and babbled something about curses and fates and bullshit, Bianca had triggered her survival mode. She kicked the table over, sending the blanket unraveling and Parker's ripening corpse rolling into Cristal. His cringing reaction to that was enough of a distraction for Bianca to snap the gun out of Cristal's hand and fire at him to keep him at bay. She motioned for me to follow her, but as I struggled to work myself free of the fallen table and tangle of bloody blankets, I noticed the body wasn't Parker's.

"Shit, this is Dutchy," I said.

"I don't care if it's Jesus Christ. Get your gun out and run."

I pulled my gun and ran after her, but I couldn't get Dutchy's face out of my mind. Where was Parker? Had he even been dead? Was he pretending to get us out of there? And who found Dutchy and brought his body to Cristal? There'd been enough people in that trailer that I wasn't really surprised, I was just more confused at why all of this was happening.

"What about the guy in the photo?" I asked Bianca

as I caught up with her.

"Mission's off," she said. "It's not like we were getting paid to do it."

"He might know something though."

"Ah," she said. "You're thinking hostage, not victim."

"Right. So should we grab him?"

She looked around the room and saw the guy from the photo standing near the stage comforting the official victim of this event who had been standing on the stage and was now covered in theatrical blood while pacing scattershot around the room.

"Cover me," Bianca said, turning back into the crowd toward where the guy was. "Make sure nobody bum rushes me while I get him."

I surveyed the room as I followed behind Bianca, mostly keeping an eye on Cristal who was still struggling to get out from under the fallen table and Dutchy's body. For a supposedly hardcore gangster, he sure seemed to get creeped out by dead bodies easily. He was finally able to push the mess of blanket and dinnerware off himself just as Bianca grabbed hold of our friend from the headshot. She pulled him by the arm as she fired off two more shots in Cristal's direction to keep him from trying to chase her down. I did the same with my gun and ran as quickly as I could to catch up.

We ran out of the ballroom and turned to head back down the main hallway we came from but saw a cluster of armed men approaching quickly. To the left, back toward where the casino's hotel lobby was, a group of security officers and tribal police was gathering, so Bianca ran straight ahead into the main casino floor. Two security guards, fat with age and laziness, made a brief attempt to stop us, but they saw the other armed factions closing in on us as well and determined they didn't need to be heroes. I'd never been in this casino before and I didn't think Bianca had either, but she navigated it like she'd been raised there. When I finally pulled up and matched Bianca's pace, she slowed down and pushed all of us off to the side.

"Get his wallet," she said to me.

"Yeah, sure, take it," the guy said. "I'm not going to—"

"You're not going to do anything," Bianca said, putting her gun to the guy's head.

I felt him pee through his pants as I dug around for his wallet. It was in his front pocket right near the splash zone. When I had it in my pocket, we were on the run again. The only thing keeping the crews on our tail from opening fire were the innocent people around us, and I didn't want to give up that advantage until we had to. Bianca seemed to be on the same page as she worked us through the most crowded parts of the gaming area— much more crowded than I would have expected in the middle of the week—heading toward a glass door at the back with signs pointing toward the outdoor theater.

Bianca was going to see her New Kids concert one way or the other, though I'm not sure how she expected to get us through the guards and the metal detectors while dragging along a hostage. And despite peeing himself, I was quite amazed with how well the hostage was handling the whole thing. He wasn't crying, he wasn't begging for his life, he was just going with the flow and not making it any harder on us than it needed to be.

What had my life come to when I was admiring a nameless hostage for handling a stressful situation better than I was?

"What's the plan, my dear?" I asked as we burst through the glass door and toward the concert crowd.

"I love this song," she said. "I know it's one of their more recent ones, but it really pumps me up."

A boy band from the eighties had recent songs? I really was out of the loop culturally. Or maybe it was only because I wasn't a girl.

"I bet this is the one they're opening with," she continued. "Gah, why couldn't the concert have been the hit target instead of the stupid murder mystery dinner?"

"Hit target?" our hostage asked. Perhaps he'd only been so calm so far because he thought he was an accidental hostage, not the focus of our murderous intent. Boy was he in for a late shocker.

"Not important now, buddy," Bianca said to him. "I don't suppose you have the keys to the van on you?"

"I don't have a van," he said. "I drive a Prius."

"That's lovely," Bianca said. "Way to look out for Mother Earth and all that. But I was talking to him."

"You know I hate that mangled lump of keys," I said. "So why would I bring it if—"

"We've got to head for the highway then," she said, pointing off to our right toward where the rolling green nature preserve ended at a major road with a giant neon eagle sat atop an even more giant neon sign for the casino.

My breathing was starting to wheeze and my stomach was cramping and knotting in alternate waves making me sick and exhausted and not at all happy about trying to keep this pace up long enough to make the longish run out to the highway.

"I don't...know," I said, gasping. "We can't just...take a car...from the—"

"We've got two guns and a hostage. We can take

167

whatever we want."

"More...importantly—"

I wasn't able to finish because my foot hit a hole in the ground, and I flipped then rolled along the ground to a stop. My ankle felt warm and began throbbing immediately. It was going to be a stretch for me to make it to the road with them prior to that, but there was no way I was going to be able to stand on my own before the swarms of armed men got to us, let alone make it all the way to the highway. So I waved them off. Bianca didn't take much convincing. She gave me a quick fist bump and a kiss on the cheek before she was off. I grabbed my ankle and looked to see if anything was poking out of the skin while I waited to see which group would get to me first and whether I would go to jail or die.

As the two teams swarmed out away from the theater and got into the open, I heard a few bursts of gunfire and the groups scattered even more. It seemed like instead of coming for me, they were too busy shooting at each other. I took that as a sign, along with my ankle that was working as well as it needed to for me to stand on my own. I didn't have any illusions about having the confidence or skill to stand in the middle of a major road and carjack someone, but the road seemed like a safer place to be than any other option available, so I hobbled and limped and wobbled as quickly as I could in that direction.

I could still hear bursts of gunfire and muted screaming from behind me, but my attention was focused on the two-tiered set of blindingly bright headlights coming my way. A smarter man would have run a different direction, but everything behind me sounded like death and everything in front of me was swimming in yellow lines and white glowing clouds, so I just stood where I was.

As the lights grew closer, I wondered if perhaps my life that had so far traversed along the boring suburban literary path followed by the scummy crime fiction path was now moving into science fiction territory with an alien encounter. At that point, an abduction by creatures from outer space was the only thing that would have surprised me as a development. But it was a spaceship. Just as I heard a growling noise and felt the ground below me rumble, as I thought the lights were going to fully engulf me and suck me away from this planet, they took a hard left and I saw Bianca doing donuts in a stacked four-by-four pickup with our hostage hanging out of the passenger's window.

"Need a ride, cowboy?"

Chapter Twenty-one

Bianca slowed down long enough for me to jump onto the back of the truck, but as she peeled off back toward the highway, I still had to work my way up a couple of levels and ladders before I was safely in the bed of the truck. I banged on the window when I finally felt like I was stable enough not to fall out of the truck and she waved at me.

We were headed straight for the highway. She motioned for me to hold onto something, which I just barely did as she swung the truck hard to the right and hit a ramp of dirt and wood that launched the truck onto the highway into oncoming traffic. She corrected quickly though and soon we had stabilized and were going with the flow of traffic not looking suspicious at all.

I knocked on the window again, trying to get her to stop so I could move into the cab of the truck, but she waved me off and sped up. I could see an onramp to the highway approaching on our right and figured that's where she would head. We'd be harder to track on a highway than we would be on the backwoods trails and roads that made up the rest of the area around the tribal land. Since I couldn't get up into the cab, I stretched myself out on the surprisingly comfortable bed of the truck. It was squishy and springy, and I wondered if it had been designed for sleeping more than carrying cargo. I wasn't able to think much about that because I quickly feel asleep.

When I opened my eyes again, Bianca was dragging me by the legs. I was disoriented from the double whammy of waking up in the back of a truck and from the flashlight she kept shining in my face, so I kicked her away and scrambled to something approaching a standing position on my own.

"Sorry, dude," she said. "Thought you passed out. Didn't realize you were just napping."

"Where are we?"

"Able's Body. Only place I could think of where we could lay low and get our heads screwed back on straight."

"Is your buddy Abbott coming?"

"I didn't call anybody. I know you think Jay knows about this place and knows we stopped, but I'm not so sure. And even if he does, I'd rather defend our position here when he comes for us than a rest stop or some fucking water park."

She made a certain amount of sense. I would have been happier staying on the run, but I'd been running for so long and was never able to get away. I'd come home to Detroit so I could stop running, but maybe it was this weird little town surrounded by windmills and an opulent temple to high school football where I would make my last stand.

I followed Bianca and her hostage into the bar, but just before we entered, she leaned into the hostage's ear and said something quietly. I figured she was probably threatening him with a painful death if he tried to run away or tell anyone in the bar what was going on, but then he smiled and she smiled and they both laughed. They didn't look back at me, but I got the queasy feeling they'd been talking about me. I'd been so worried about being betrayed by Jay and his family or by the cops we were working with, but I wondered if I needed to worry about being betrayed by my alleged partner in crime. Could she have been the one to tip off Cristal where I was? I know they had a romantic history and his aunt had talked favorably about them together, but what did she stand to gain from that? Having Cristal in the mix made taking out Jay's family harder. Was she lying about wanting revenge for her father's death?

Oh, god. Was she even related to him? I hadn't done background checks on everyone involved, the parties and alliances just seemed to fall along natural lines, despite how unnatural all of this was. There was no way this could turn out good for me. I didn't even want to step into the bar. It felt like enemy territory more than a safe zone. What I should have done was taken the keys from Bianca, jumped in that truck, and driven away as far as I could. I knew I couldn't keep running, but I could run to someplace where I wasn't being set up. Where my alleged partner wasn't laughing secretly at me with her fucking hostage.

Where my ears weren't buzzing incessantly from those goddamn windmills. How did people live like that every day?

But I didn't know where Bianca was keeping the keys to the truck, I really didn't know where else I would go, and, most importantly, I wanted to find out why Jay wanted this guy dead.

So I followed them into the bar and told myself there were any number other things they could have been laughing about.

Bianca ordered us a round of sodas and chicken wings, then said, "Well let's get this fella's wallet out and see who we're traveling with."

Dammit, the wallet. I'd had a great bit of leverage in my pocket the whole time and completely forgot about it. I pulled it out and the guy snatched it away from me.

"I'll tell you whatever you want to know," he said. "You don't have to invade my privacy."

"Got something in there you don't want us to see?" I asked.

He gripped the wallet tighter and pulled it closer to his body.

"A wallet is a man's private space, come on. I said, I'll tell you whatever you want to know."

"How do we know you'll tell us the truth?"

"You've got guns. Why the hell would I lie?"

"Man's got a point," Bianca said.

"Whatever," I said, immediately wishing it hadn't come out as petty and pathetic sounding as it had.

"Let's start with the name, then, hostage boy."

"Martin Nelson. Marty."

"Job?"

"Actor and principal owner of Murder for Hire Production."

"Murder for hire?"

"Dinner theater shows, corporate retreats, holiday parties, that sort of thing. Not what you two do."

"What do we do?"

"You're hired guns, right?"

173

I opened my mouth to clarify our roles when Bianca held her hand out and snapped at my face.

"We're not talking about us right now. We're getting to know you, our new friend. So you own this company? Where'd you get the money?"

"I sold a trilogy of paperback original serial killer novels back in 2008, right before the big crash that killed the publishing industry."

"How did the publishing industry crashing lead to you owning a mystery dinner company?" I asked, genuinely interested.

"They didn't publish the book but they still had to pay me. So I got the money for all three books at once and while the money was nice, I really wanted to see my work out there, and this opportunity presented itself through a friend of mine from college theater and here we are."

I wanted to ask him how much he'd been paid for the books, but I was afraid of the answer. And Bianca redirected the conversation back toward our main goal anyway, so I was saved.

"What we're really trying to find out," she said, quieting her voice as the waitress approached to drop off our food, "is why someone was trying to kill you?"

"You don't know why you're supposed to kill me?"

"Dammit," Bianca said. "I told you we're the ones asking questions. Nobody said we're supposed to kill you. If we were supposed to kill you, don't you think you'd be dead?"

He shrugged and took a chicken wing from the pile in the middle of the table. He seemed pretty cocky for a guy who peed on my hand through his pants the first time Bianca put a gun to his head.

"Not if you don't know *why* you're supposed to kill me," he said, following the chicken wing with a long slurp from his soda.

We were the only ones in the bar other than the bartender and the waitress, and I could tell Bianca wanted to drag this guy across the table and pistol whip him, but she kept her cool and kept her gun hidden.

"There may be people watching now," she said, slowly. "But they're not going to be here forever. Eventually they'll close the place down and go home and we'll be here all alone. And I'll remember every little thing you've done to piss me off, and how do you think that'll turn out for you?"

Even though Nelson's body went slack and he seemed to relax, I could see a twitch in the corner of his lips and a widening of his eyes that indicated he was still pretty freaked out. And who could blame him? That didn't mean we could go easy on him though. He wasn't our friend. Well, he wasn't my friend. I was beginning to wonder if I had any idea at all who Bianca considered her friends.

"If I had to guess," Nelson said, "I'd probably say my dad would be behind any plan to...deal with me."

"Your father?"

Bianca's look of horror made me doubt my earlier questions about her own fatherly relationship to this mess.

"Foster father, stepfather, not sure what to actually call him, but he's the one who raised me and took responsibility for me and made me who I am...or who I was, before the acting stuff."

"He wants to kill you because you're an actor?"

"Because I'm an embarrassment to the tribe and to his...professional associates."

175

"Tribe? Like the casino Indians?"

"Chippewa, they run the Pleasantwood reservation and my dad, er, my...Bill, is on the tribal council but his big deal is with the jails and stuff on the reservation. I think there's even a tribal—"

"Jails?" I asked. "Shit. Like corrections?"

"He tried to explain it to me once—I think he always hoped I'd give up my artistic ambitions and join the tribal police force one day to keep his business going."

"Explain what?" I asked, trying to keep my patience in check.

"The tribe up here is small, three thousand or so, I think, and they have one jail and a bunch of cops who only became cops so they can shake down tourists and tribal members they have a problem with. But the BIA has been pushing to take over the jails and—"

"BIA?"

"Bureau of Indian Affairs. The most hated organization ever among these people."

"Do you know the name Jay Taylor?" I asked.

"Doesn't ring a bell, but like I said, after that big talk where he tried to direct my future path and I rebuffed him, I've kind of tuned out on family business."

"This has to be it," I said to Bianca.

"It does seem to fit..."

"What seems to fit? What's going on."

Bianca put her arm on his shoulder and Nelson freaked out. I think he thought she was legit going to kill him right there.

"Shit, I didn't mean to ask questions again. I'm just curious. If he wasn't such an asshole, I would have loved to work more with my dad. It sounds like what he did was cool, at least the parts that didn't involve killing people."

"The guy who hired us to kill you is Jay Taylor, my ex-wife's sort of brother. He runs what's left of a criminal enterprise based out of the Michigan Department of Corrections and her dad was a Secret Service agent that was investigating an identity theft ring in the prisons."

He seemed to understand what I was saying, so I kept going.

"So we're guessing that your…Bill…was working with Jay to somehow hold off the BIA taking over the tribal jails and crushing his own little criminal enterprise."

"So we have our answer," Bianca said, "but still don't know anything."

"Sounds about right," I said. "But I think we have some leverage with our new friend here."

"Leverage? I don't like the sound of that."

His relaxed body clenched again and he looked like he was ready to take a dump right there in the bar.

"Leverage is better than target, isn't?" Bianca asked, rubbing Nelson's shoulders with the hands that had initially been ready to strangle him.

"But I don't know anything."

"Leave that part to us," I said. "We're both kind of experts at convincing people we know way more than we really do."

Bianca nodded in agreement, though she gave me a bit of a side-eye look as she did it that told me she wasn't totally buying what I was selling. It didn't matter right then though as we had a new goal: instead of killing Martin Nelson, we would keep him alive long enough to get him to someone with the power and savvy to tap into whatever knowledge he had about Jay's plan to thwart the BIA. I thought that person could be Theo

Abbott until he crashed into the bar with his car and opened fire.

Chapter Twenty-two

After a round of screaming and diving for cover, the gunfire stopped almost as quickly as it had started, but nobody came out of hiding until we were all sure there wasn't a second wave of gunfire waiting for us. Bianca was the first to emerge from the behind the bar. She kept her gun pointed at the driver's side of the car as she slowly approached the steaming knot of glass and metal where the front wall of the bar had once been.

"Looks like he killed himself," she said, putting her gun away.

"It's Abbott?"

"I don't get it. Where's the other guy?"

"Herren," I said. "He's the one I thought would bring this whole thing down."

"You know this guy?" Nelson asked, peeking his head up over the bar as well.

"There was something off when we met them," Bianca said. "Teddy seemed weird around that guy and I'd never seen him before in my life."

I came out from behind the bar and joined her as she moved back and forth around the space occupied by the front end of the car and Abbott's body. I wasn't comfortable enough to put my gun away and had it at my side as I walked.

"You think he was compromised?"

"I'm starting to think everybody was compromised," she said. "Which means we're all fucked."

"It's like a western," I said. "And this can be our last stand. We just wait for word to spread to all the bad guys that this is where we can be found and as they come for us, we kill them."

"And if they all come for us at once?"

"We go down in a blaze of glory."

"I don't like this plan at all," Nelson said. "I'm too young for a blaze of glory. I want real glory. I want—"

Bianca held her hand up again to quiet him.

"I've never been much of the waiting sort," she said. "I think there's another way."

"Go after the head?" I asked.

"Head, foot, legs, arms, wings, all of them. We show up, shoot whoever's there, and move on until we're caught or killed."

"Again, I hate to be the down voice," Nelson said. "But I don't like all of these sacrificial plans."

"You're not giving us a ton to work with, kid. So we're going with what we know."

"All the stuff you're talking about, that's all state shit, right?"

"Secret Service was federal, but I'm listening."

"The only thing more powerful than the state is the federal government."

"The BIA?"

"I have no loyalty to the tribe," he said. "And I'd love to see somebody knock Bill's ass down a peg or two."

"And you say you have no idea why anyone would want to kill you," I said.

Bianca glared at me.

"I'm an asshole, sure," he said. "But if that's an executable offense, we're all screwed."

The boy had a point.

As I followed Bianca around the wreckage of the car and the wall, I could clearly see why she assumed Abbott had killed himself. There was a chunk missing from his head on the side of his body holding a handgun. It was certainly possible that someone had been in the car with him and somehow managed to shoot him on the opposite side of his head and then somehow escape before the car crashed into the bar. Possible, but not probable.

I was thinking about that mysterious assassin passenger when Nelson finally made his way out from behind the bar and over to the wreckage. I'd learned quite a bit about the Department of Corrections as I planned for my eventual takedown of the family, and I'd never come across Herren's name. And Bianca knew enough about her dad's work that she should have known Herren's name if he was really working as closely with her dad's best buddy as Abbott was making it out like they were.

Which only meant one thing.

"Did your dad ever mention a guy named Greg Herren?" I asked Nelson, spinning him away from the car's wreckage.

"Uh...that one does kind of ring a bell."

I smiled and looked to see if Bianca had heard; she was still staring into the car at Abbott's body, probably having something of a traumatic reimagining of her dad's death. I wanted to wave her over and let her in on this new direction that was developing, but she seemed

181

lost in her grief and I didn't want to break that up. Since she hadn't been there, I guessed she hadn't had the time to process it fully in a way that was healthy for her to move on.

I was in no shape to help, so I made small talk with Nelson about being part of the Native American community in Michigan while I waited for Bianca to finish up. We'd worked our way through most of the least offensive topics of discussion related to Native Americans when she made her way over to us.

"I don't think Gregg Herren was with Corrections. I think he was Jay's guy in the Bureau of Indian Affairs."

"Maybe," Bianca said. "But they were fighting the BIA, so why would they have a man from BIA on their team? Herren was squirrely, but nothing about him said government guy to me."

"If I remember right, I think they were talking to some of the bigger tribes out west who have their own tribal departments of correction," Nelson said. "Maybe that's who he was."

I slapped him on the back and Bianca went in for a high five.

"Now that's how you go from hostage to partner real quick," she said. "Hot damn."

"Again, though," I said. "We have more information, but we still don't know anything. And we still have at least three distinct factions on our tail that will probably be arriving here any time now to kill slash jail us."

"Ugh," Bianca said. "You and your facts. He's right though, god help us all, so let's saddle up, boys."

We were back in the truck and on the road—with me riding shotgun this time—soon after, headed back toward Detroit. We still hadn't decided what we were going to do with Nelson and his information, but we were still locked in on keeping him alive and the best chances for that were away from where we'd been. As much as I liked the thought of sheltering in place and picking off those that would come for us one at a time, we had no assurances they even knew where we were or that they would attack soon. I'd been getting better at having patience, but I wasn't to the point where I could hide out in a small town bar for months on end waiting for gangsters to attack.

"You know," Nelson said from the back seat about an hour into the drive, "when Bill wanted to get in front of something he didn't understand fully but knew big pieces of, he'd hold a press conference. He'd drop the big chunks he knew about something and then use his contacts in the media to see what shook loose that helped fill in the blanks."

"That can give us a deadline too," I said.

"Right," Bianca said. "Instead of holing up in town there and waiting until who knows when for folks to show up and attack us, we go on TV, say we have information about a massive criminal enterprise working in the state Department of Corrections and the tribal law enforcement community, then give them a time and place when we'll put Martin Nelson in front of a microphone to make a statement and answer some questions—"

"I can't answer any questions. I really don't know much about what's going on."

"Honey," Bianca said, "if that press conference actually happens, we'll have more than your lack of knowledge to worry about."

"You're the bait to draw all the people who want to kill us out of hiding so we can go on the offensive."

"Yay," Nelson said. "Can I just go back to being leverage instead of bait?"

"So where do we hide out until we can get him on camera?"

"Hide?" Bianca asked. "We won't be hiding. We'll be camped out right on their fucking doorstep."

"Jay's house?"

She nodded. "Jay's house."

Chapter Twenty-three

"There's a guest house in the back where we can crash while we figure out the logistics of all of this," I said as we exited the expressway into the lakefront jewel of the Detroit area, St. Clair Shores.

"What didn't you get the first time we talked through this?" Bianca asked, in what I thought was an unnecessarily harsh tone. It was one more brick in the wall of women I'd let into my life as friends and lovers who eventually turned into nagging mothers.

"I know we want them to come to us and we don't want to wait around for it too long, but we aren't going to just pull up to the main entrance and camp out in the living room while we set up these press conferences."

"Well of course not," she said. "I need a nap and I don't like to sleep on couches. We'll set up in the master bedroom."

That sounded like the worst idea ever and I told her so. Over and over and over again, even as we pulled up to the main entrance of the house.

"Are we just going to leave the truck here?"

"Gas tank's full, I think. Might make a nice rolling

bomb if it comes to that."

"I don't like this at all."

"Then you can leave any time. If you have a better idea that accomplishes our goal more efficiently or more securely, I am all ears."

"I think maybe first we should clarify what both of us mean by 'goals.'"

"Goals," she said. "Something to aim for. Hoped for outcome. You're the word guy. I didn't think I'd need to give you vocabulary lessons."

"Stop being a bitch. You know what I mean."

"I'm not sure I do. I thought we were on the same page, but it seems like every time we talk about this, the goalposts change."

"You want revenge on Jay Taylor and anyone around him who was responsible for pushing your dad to suicide. And I want to put a bullet between Jay's eyes so I can move through the rest of my life freely without always looking over my shoulder wondering if he's sending someone else after me."

"There we go then. Squad goals."

"Oh, god. What a horrible trendy phrase," I said, sounding every bit the old man I felt like. "Don't ever say that again."

"I can't say I feel particularly ecstatic about any of the plans mentioned to protect me. In fact, I've heard lots of plans and pieces of plans that use me, but that make no efforts to protect me."

"Of course we'll protect you," Bianca said.

"If you die, nobody will watch our press conferences," I said, smiling.

I waited for him to punch me, but he just opened his door and jumped out of the truck.

"Nice place," he said. "Not the worst house to die in."

"Come on, we don't do passive-aggressive around here. If you're feeling pissy, get it out."

"Or I could just leave."

I was running a number of responses through my head ranging from witty to sincere and emotional, trying to find the right match for the moment, but Bianca was way ahead of me. She jumped out of the truck right after Nelson, grabbed him by the collar of his shirt, and rammed the gun into his left eye socket.

"I apologize if anything we've said on the ride here or before that gave you the impression that you were anything but a fucking hostage right now, but that's what you are. A lucky fucking hostage who should have been a smear on the fake wood paneling of that casino putting on your precious murder mystery theater. I will keep you alive because it makes what I want to do easier. But do not ever think you are important enough to me and what I want to do that I won't kill you just to make a point. Do you understand?"

He shook his head a little bit, but his movements were hampered by her grip on his collar and, what I assumed, was the sheer terror running through his mind.

"I said do you fucking understand."

"Yes, ma'am."

She let go of his collar and pushed him away then pointed the gun at men.

"Same goes for you. Are we clear?"

I was dumb, but not dumb enough to argue with her right then, so I also said, "Yes, ma'am."

"I know many people will think this is just a stunt,"

187

Nelson said, as his first appearance in front of the cameras came to a close. "And I guess in many ways, it is. But that doesn't mean that what I'm saying should matter any less or that what I'm saying is any less true. All I'm asking for is for folks to listen to my story and then do their own research to verify that what I'm saying is true."

After he was done speaking, there was a loud wave of sound made up of all of the reporters' questions that cascaded from the news crews standing on Jay's front lawn, and Nelson ignored them all and followed us back up to the master bedroom. As Bianca and Nelson chatted about the press conference, I looked out the window onto the lawn and saw that they were all still there. I'd expected they would see Nelson's performance, get intrigued by the little bit he had dropped, then rush back to their studios and newsrooms and start digging up whatever they could on the folks involved. If we were going to have to deal with a swarm of paparazzi on the lawn the whole time we were there, it would throw our plan for a nasty loop. Nobody would want to attack the house in front of a gaggle of news cameras and reporters.

We'd been there for roughly twenty-four hours and hadn't seen any sign of Jay or the rest of the family. I could never get around to calling them my family, which was fine, but I worried it didn't mean enough for what I was feeling if it wasn't family. I flopped onto the bed, debriefing myself internally, when the phone at the desk in the bedroom rang. I wasn't sure if I should answer it, considering it wasn't my house and all, but it kept ringing and kept ringing and Bianca glared at me and motioned for me to pick it up.

"If you're not out of that house by tomorrow morning," Jay said, before I even had the receiver fully to my ear, "I'll blow up the entire place, reporters and all."

"Wrong number," I said.

I smiled at Bianca as I hung up, but I knew he would do it and knew I'd probably survive and have to deal with all those innocent lives on my conscience in addition to all the others with more flexible innocence.

"Who was that?"

"In this day and age," I said, bypassing her question while I tried to work out in my head what my next move should be, "I'm always shocked when I find people who have a land line. I mean sure, old people like them because they like to talk to random telemarketers who—"

"Who was on the phone, Dominick?"

"I said, it was a wrong—"

"What did Jay say?" She asked.

I looked at Nelson then back to Bianca and couldn't think of any good reason not to tell them.

"He said if we're not out of here by tomorrow morning he's going to blow the house up with us in it and probably take out all the reporters too."

Nelson's face went whiter than chalk sculpture and I thought for a second there he was going to throw up. I would have enjoyed seeing that, especially if he got it all over Jay's fancy bedding, but Bianca didn't seem to think the news was all that troubling.

"Bullshit," in fact, is what she said.

"This family has never been the type to get sentimental about property," I said, moving off the bed and out of Nelson's vomit range. "I think they keep extra houses just so they can threaten to blow them up for effect."

"How, though? Does he have a remote detonator? A grenade launcher? Do they build all of their family homes with pipe bombs next to the HVAC system?"

"Well, I guess probably no, but I also wouldn't put it past—"

"He's desperate and he's trying to get into your head," she said. "Keep him out."

I agreed and went back to the window to see if the reporters were still there or if they'd just been taking their time leaving, but the camp was still there and I think it was even getting bigger.

"Just in case though," Bianca said, "why don't you and Nelson go have a look around and see if anything looks shady."

Chapter Twenty-four

The house wasn't the biggest I'd ever seen, and it wasn't even the biggest house on its street, but it was big enough and virtually impossible to look through completely. We'd already been through it once when we arrived. We wanted to make sure no one was hiding and that there weren't any stray family members or kids that had been left behind, and we also made ourselves a meal to recharge after quite the draining previous day. But we hadn't taken the time to do a full top-to-bottom search for strategic purposes.

There was one big main chunk in the center with a two-story living room that looked out over the water with a giant fireplace and TV in the middle of a wall of windows, a bathroom, a small kitchen, and a den. Then there was another wing off to each side of that chunk—one wing with a bunch of bedroom, and the other with the formal rooms anyone who'd ever played Clue would recognize: the library, the formal dining room, the full kitchen, the conservatory—no really, this house had a conservatory. I thought briefly about splitting up, but I remembered Bianca's speech about Nelson being a hostage, not a friend or a partner, so I patted by pants to make sure my gun was still there and kept him close by as I gave him a speech of my own.

"I don't think it's any secret Bianca and I do things differently from each other," I said, trying to look him in the eye and keep walking at the same time. "So I'm not going to threaten you or put a gun to your head or anything like that."

"I'd take it from you if you did," he said, quickening his step.

"Listen, you little shit, I might not be a bruiser like Bianca, but don't—"

"Settle down, man. I'm kidding. Sort of. I take Krav Maga classes back in New York where I'm living now because it helps with the combat aspects of what I do with the mystery dinners. It also makes me feel more confident living my life as I see fit without worrying about some jackass thinking I'm a target because of how I look or how I walk or how I talk."

"Wait, are you saying you take Krav Maga because you're gay?"

He finally stopped walking and turned to face me. "I'm *saying*, my sexuality is my business, but if you try to put a gun in my face I'll break your hand off and smack you with it, then stick the gun where only a surgeon will be able to find it."

I gave him a fake salute and pushed in front of him to finish the walkthrough of the house. Unable to help myself, I looked back once to see if he was laughing it off, but he just had a smug smirk on his face knowing he'd set up camp in my head as well. Some fucking hostage.

I'd gotten the sense after the first time through the house that, while not abandoned, the place wasn't being used as anyone's primary residence. Working our way through it a second time only served to confirm that.

"Doesn't look like anybody's lived here for a while," I said, trying to put his last comment out of my mind and maintain my professionalism.

"It's clean," he said, "but yeah, I don't see any personal touches or any signs of people living here at all."

Working together in silence that started off awkward but gradually morphed into something more comfortable, we cleared the entire house in under an hour and both agreed that Jay was likely putting us on about being able to blow the house up.

"Though I wouldn't put it past him to use a rocket launcher," I said to Bianca when we recapped our search to her back in the bedroom.

I couldn't help but look out the window again to see if the crowd of reporters was still there and if it had gotten any larger. The group didn't seem to have gotten any bigger and it did seem like it had thinned out a bit, but there were still enough of them there to ruin our plan. I had a different plan in mind though, and they would still be a problem, but not as big of one if Bianca went along with it. I told her we needed to talk alone and Nelson rolled his eyes.

"You can leave me alone," he said. "Right now this is the safest place for me. If I run, they'll find me and there won't be a gaggle of TV cameras to record it and keep them honest. Go have your little talk. I'll stay right here like a good little hostage."

Bianca seemed reluctant to leave him alone in the bedroom, but I finally talked her into following me to the living room.

"As we walked through the house, my mind wandered a bit, as it tends to do, and I realized there are a few loose ends we need to deal with."

"Listen to you talking like a hard ass now," Bianca said, grabbing my arm excitedly like she had that first time we saw the New York City skyline together on the FDR. "Who are the loose ends we need to deal with?"

"Not who, what. Things we forgot about. Like the rental car, for one thing. You put that on your card, didn't you? Shouldn't we go get it so—"

"All this time you've known me and seen me in my element and you really think I'd rent a fucking minivan I was going to drive to a hit job under my own name and with my own credit card?"

"You used a fake card?"

"I always use a fake card. I love fake identities. It makes life so much more fun."

"But how do you—"

"Jesus, you really haven't been paying attention, have you?"

"I..."

"My dad was a Secret Service agent specializing in identity theft. He showed me everything he ever learned about spotting fakes. And in paying attention to his career and listening in the way only daddy's little girl can listen, I figured out who did the best work and how to get it without paying for it."

"Wow," I said. "Okay then, the other loose end is a vehicle as well, but not as easily solved by a fake ID."

"Okay..."

"I know neither of us is particularly detail oriented, preferring more to focus on big picture stuff and working better with our skills in improvisation, but as I was thinking about the casino debacle, I realized we let a detail slip that is so huge, I wanted to jump out the window and hit the pavement with my head because I felt so stupid."

"If this is a lesson in storytelling, I'm impressed," Bianca said. "But I'm not in the mood for a story right now so get to the fucking point."

"We left a duffel bag full of cash that we stole from Cristal Hate in the trunk of your car when Jay and his goons stopped us and threw us in their van."

"No way, that's too stupid even for…"

"Even for what? You're realizing it now too, aren't you?"

"Shit."

"There are two possibilities, neither of which are perfect, but one is more not perfect than the other."

"There's that wizardly way with words again," she said. "Just hurry up and get to it so we can start planning our next move."

"Jay wanted us, I don't think he cared about our car," I said. "At the time, I don't think he knew about the money. He may not even know right now, though I wonder if Cristal went to him to find out where I was."

Bianca waved her hands in a rolling motion indicating I should get on with the rest of my story.

"If he didn't know about the money, I don't think he'd search our car."

"You think he had it towed?"

"Maybe. I've considered both scenarios—that he had it towed to an impound lot or that he had it towed here."

"If he towed it here than we'd be—"

"I checked the garage and didn't see it in there. He still could've towed it here, but it's not likely."

"This isn't his house though, right? Maybe he had it towed to his house."

"Possible. And probably the second worst of the possibilities."

"Second worst?"

"If he really didn't care about the car at all, I don't think he would bother towing it."

"You think he just left it on the side of the road? That would be great. We could go get it right now. Let's go get it right now. We can be in Mexico in—"

"The chunk of highway he pulled us over in isn't the best part of town and that car of yours looked pretty nice."

"You think somebody stole it?"

"That's the first worst of the possibilities, yeah."

"Shit. *Shit.* How could we forget money like that?"

"We've had a lot on our minds."

"Still. That's three million things we should have had on our mind. What do we do?"

"I say we go look for the car first," I said. "See which of the scenarios we're dealing with and then go from there."

"Okay. I'm game for that. What about our hostage?"

"If we can get the money, do we really need him?"

She shrugged and chewed the inside of her mouth. "Probably not, but if this doesn't work out well, he's our only other bit of leverage."

"And I think we both know the odds of this working out well are—"

"The odds are shit. So we bring him along."

"And if the money is there?"

"We let him go."

"Without any of the money?"

"True. Think we can check for the money without letting him in on it?"

"Maybe," I said. "But he seems to have a pretty good bullshit detector. And neither of us is a good enough actor to pass muster with a professional, even a professional dinner theater actor."

"So we cut him in?"

"I'm fine with that. Even a fraction of that money would be enough to get us out of town and somewhere safe. Especially if you can get us new IDs as easy as you claim."

"Lot of talk about us," she said, standing and stretching her arms over her head. "You think that's smart, tying ourselves to each other?"

"Probably not, and if there was any way I could think of to get out of this without you at this point, I'd take it. But here we are. Go team."

"We both know you need me, but I'm a little more hazy on why I need you."

"You probably don't, but you've stuck with me this long for a reason, so I suspect you don't want to do this alone and I'm the devil you know and you assume you can be leader in a team that includes me."

"Maybe. Maybe. But also maybe I can trade you in for Martin Nelson. He seems like a pretty substantial upgrade."

"He does Krav Maga back in New York where he's living because it helps him with his acting and because it makes him feel safer. He threatened to snap off my hand and give me a colonoscopy with my own gun if I tried to do to him what you did."

"It's settled then. I'm upgrading to Nelson. It's been fun."

I smiled and held out my hand for a handshake. "Good luck, then."

197

I kept my hand outstretched much longer than I expected I would have to and she never took it. Finally, she swatted my hand away and started back toward the stairs.

"Much as I would love to dump you, I know you'd be back and back and back again, always at the worst possible times and I'd never be able to enjoy the money. So let's go get out hostage and see if the two of us can manage to act smooth enough to outsmart the Al Pacino of murder mystery dinner theater."

Chapter Twenty-five

The car was still on the side of the road, so we passed by it once, looking for traps, then doubled back around to pull off the side of the road on the opposite side of the highway.

"Explain again what we're doing here," Nelson said.

"What you're doing out here is being a good boy and keeping your mouth shut while we do a little investigating," Bianca said.

"Enough of the patronizing bullshit. You guys are up to something and I want to know what it is."

"Fine, you caught us," I said. "We're looking for places to hide your body when this all goes to hell."

"What did I tell you back at the house? She can get away with that stuff but you—"

"Both of you stop it," Bianca said. "You and I are going to stay in the truck, Nelson, and Dominick is going to go and check out the car. Are we all clear?"

"Did anyone check this truck for weapons?" I asked. "It seems like the sort of truck that would have guns on board."

"There are no guns. Go search the car."

199

I started my search inside the car because I didn't want to clue Nelson in on what kind of item we were looking for. If I went right to the trunk, he'd know we were looking for something big and would get too curious. I started with the glovebox and looked under the seats and all around the interior of the car before moving to the trunk. I also rolled under the car and looked as much as I could in the wheel wells and the undercarriage. It was a Mini Cooper though, which meant it was lower to the ground and didn't have much area underneath to explore. Everything I'd seen inside the car made me confident that no one had touched it and that the bag of money would still be in the trunk when I looked.

I was not disappointed.

The duffle bag was right where I left it. I reached in to grab it but stopped before hauling out it. Was it really going to be this easy? This had to be a trap. How could this have been sitting alongside of the road for so long without being taken. There were no stickers on the car indicating the car had been tagged by the police for removal for being on the side of the road for too long. As I thought about it though, it made more sense. Everything that had happened since we'd been pulled over felt like it had taken place over weeks, but in reality, it hadn't even been thirty-six hours. So I grabbed the bag, didn't care if Nelson figured out what it was, and hiked across the highway back to the truck. I tossed the bag on the passenger's side floor and climbed in after it.

"Wait," Bianca said. "I've had a change of heart."

I didn't like the sound of that at all. My stomach clenched and I flexed my leg and back muscles to confirm my gun was still on me. But this wasn't a double-cross. She was setting Nelson free.

"I've got a spare key hidden under my car over there, so you can keep the truck and take it back to the casino and trade it for your car and be on your way."

"What's in the bag?"

"Luggage. Are you ready to go?"

"Bullshit. You were going to kill me and then you were going to use me as live bait, but then suddenly you get this magical—"

In one swift move, Bianca pulled her gun and swung around and shot Nelson once in the head then pointed the gun at me.

"I should have done this sooner, but I'm walking away. You'll survive, you always do."

She kept her gun trained on my chest as she reached over and unzipped the duffel bag with her other hand. It unzipped easily at first, but then stuck and she had trouble getting it open.

"Shit," she said. "Finish unzipping that for me and take a handful or two out for yourself then I'll be on my way."

I was going to argue, but there was no point. My fight was gone, and I already had plenty of blood money in my bank account if I really wanted to use it. So I grabbed a few handfuls, dropped them on the floor, and zipped the bag back up. Bianca tugged it out after her and ran across the street to her car and drove away.

And that was that. I sat in the passenger's seat, surround by the bills I'd dropped, unsure what to do next. I didn't want to drive the truck anywhere. I wasn't sure I'd be able to do it even if I had the desire. I didn't want to chase after her because she'd obviously made up her mind and she was right. I would survive. At first, I'd be afraid, I'd be petrified...

I looked in the rearview mirror and what was left of Martin Nelson's body dominated my line of sight. Blood and brains coated the back windshield creating kind of a gooey stained glass look in the back of the truck that would have been cool looking to someone who didn't know how the look was achieved.

"Sometimes during allergy season, I'd love to be head-free like that," I said to the headless lump. "During the worst of it, there's always a time, usually the dead of January or February, when I'm tempted to just grab a drill and open up my head and let the snot free. I'm guess that won't be a problem for you."

The keys were still in the ignition even though Bianca had turned the truck off. I turned the key to the auxiliary position and switched the radio on.

"Not sure what your music preference is, probably show tunes or classical or something fancy like that, but in a truck like this it only seems fitting to listen to country."

When the radio crackled to life, it was set on a conservative AM talk radio station that was popular in the area for its nutty hosts and doomsday prepper supply advertisers. I pushed the button for satellite radio and was immediately assaulted by a bro country song of the worst order.

"That doesn't count as country," I said. "I'm all for expanding the form, but there should never be rap in country music."

Martin Nelson's body slumped further into the seat and I took that as implied agreement with what I said. I tuned the station up a few numbers to the outlaw country station and was rewarded with Waylon Jennings singing "Are You Sure Hank Done It This Way."

"Now this is country music," I said. "And it has the

added bonus of being sorta meta about the music business. The only thing I like more than books about writers is country songs about country singers."

There was a string of four or five good songs on the station, then I switched it over the Broadway station in honor of Nelson, before turning it back to the country station. I don't know how long I'd been sitting there, my sense of time was even more skewed in that truck than it had been otherwise, but I heard someone pull up behind the truck and assumed it was the police. Or Jay. Or Greg Herren. Or Cristal Hate. Or someone else from my past who had a beef with me that I'd completely forgotten about.

The person I didn't expect to see was Bianca. And I really didn't expect her to throw the bag of money into the driver's seat and say, "It's all counterfeit."

"All of it?"

I picked up one of the handfuls from the floor in front of me and looked through it. It didn't look counterfeit to me, but unless it had a cartoon character on it or was printed on neon-colored paper, I wouldn't have noticed it. But I suspected Bianca's instincts on this were as fine-tuned as her ID sense.

"I didn't look through all the bills," she said. "But I looked through enough to think the whole mess is funny money."

"You think it was like that when I took it?"

"I don't know?"

"You think maybe it's been fake all along and even Cristal didn't notice?"

"I don't *know*."

"But if he knew, why would he come all the way up to the casino to attack us and get back his counterfeit money?"

"I. Don't. KNOW."

I wanted to ask her where she thought Parker's body had gone to and if maybe he was still alive, but she made it very clear she was not interested in further discussion, so I let it go. I pulled the bag out of the front seat and threw it in the back next to Nelson's body.

"Counterfeit, can you believe that?" I said to him.

Bianca looked at me like I'd pulled my pants down in front of her and mooned a bus of nuns.

"Who are you talking to?"

"After you left, Mr. Nelson and I had quite the bonding experience talking about music," I said. "And I think I know him well enough now that I'm certain he'd be interested in knowing this money was counterfeit."

Bianca rolled her eyes and started the truck back up. I leaned over and whispered in her ear, "You should have heard the horrible things he said about you after you left us here."

I looked back at Nelson when I was done and shrugged.

"You had to know I was going to tell her," I said. "It was some pretty awful stuff."

After revving the engine a few times, Bianca put the truck in gear and roared across six lanes of traffic before coming to a stop on the opposite side of the road. She looked at me a couple of times and I could tell she was trying to figure out if being alone in the truck with a headless corpse had finally snapped whatever fragile threads of sanity I had left. I'd been trying to figure the same thing out myself and hadn't reached a verifiable conclusion yet.

"While you two are chatting, can you rip off his shirt

or whatever part of it you can? I need something long enough to use as a fuse."

"Fuse?"

"Get the shirt. You'll see."

Even though the gunshot had made a mess of Nelson's head and the surrounding walls and windows, it had left the rest of his body intact. That made unbuttoning his dress shirt and getting it off him an almost impossible task. After a few tries and a few more times of almost sticking my hand in the squishy remains of his noggin, I gave up and took off my own shirt. I had an undershirt on so I wasn't topless as I handed the shirt to Bianca.

"You want to light or you want to drive?"

"You're the driver," I said. "I've crashed go-karts."

She grunted and handed me a lighter and the shirt then jumped back into the truck. As she moved the truck around so it was pointing down toward a hill off the side of the highway, she was yelling instructions to me.

"Roll the shirt up as tightly as you can and then shove it into the gas tank. We're lucky this truck still has one of those old-school gas tanks big enough to fit a rag in."

I wrapped it tightly and crammed it as far into the gas tank as I could while Bianca wriggled out of the truck.

"This next part is very important," she said as the truck stopped again. "I can't have you spacing out on me here, okay? I need you to light that shirt and let it burn until the fire is *almost* to the gas tank and then yell at me to let go. If you yell too soon, the fire will burn out and this won't work and if you don't yell soon enough, it'll go boom while we're standing next to it and send us all to the eternal place of burning together."

I knew she was joking, but that was the first time I really thought about my place in the afterlife. Hell. I'd been so worried about surviving forever on this planet with the weight of my sins needling me every day, I hadn't even considered spending eternity in hell. It would have been easier if I didn't believe and I could just convince myself that once this life was over that was it, but I knew better. I knew Hell was real and hoped I'd get a chance for forgiveness before finding myself in the new arrival line down there.

"I got it," I said, lighting the shirt.

When the time was right, I yelled her name. She started the truck rolling down the hill and flew from the driver's side just in time to clear the blast zone as the truck went up in flames so amazing I wondered if she had worked with a special effects team. I ran to meet her, but she waved me across the street to her car.

"You drive," she said, holding out her keys to me. "I need to call Jay and tell him we killed his mark and call Cristal and tell him we have his money."

"I thought we talked about this already," I said, waving off the keys—I flashed back to the wad of minivan rental keys digging into my leg earlier and that triggered a quick succession of flash visions: Parker yelling at me, Parker coming at me with a Taser, Parker gurgling when Bianca stabbed him. "You're the driver and I'm the—"

"This isn't a fucking discussion, Dominick. I stabbed a guy, I shot a guy, and I saw one of the most revered father figures in my life crash through a bar and blow his brains out in front of me. Pardon me if I feel like I'm not fit to operate a three-ton death machine right now."

I wanted to keep arguing with her. I was feeling my own bit of hesitation of getting behind the wheel, but Bianca would do a better job with the phone calls, making Jay and the others think we were really going to offer up the money and not give away anything in her tone. So I took the keys in the most grandiose fashion I could muster and pretended I was taking a Sunday drive with my best gal, not driving the getaway car for the devil.

Chapter Twenty-six

Bianca called Jay first and I could hear him screaming through the speaker. He calmed down after a few seconds and I could only hear Bianca's side of the conversation. It felt weird to be in the passenger's seat, both literally and figuratively, as someone else plotted my final confrontation with the big boss at the end of the video game that was my life.

I expected to feel the same thing when she called Cristal, too, but with Jay it felt like she was invading my territory and taking over my life's quest. And yet, I didn't stop her. I had to admit, in that moment, I hoped they would all show up and Bianca would kill them and make my life easier without me having to deal with the ramifications of being the shooter. But that was just another form of running away and I was done running away. I kept telling myself that, even though I didn't seem inclined to listen to myself, knowing that it would only take once for me to get it right and make it stick.

She made the same call to Cristal with the same basic results, only more screaming and more creative cursing, and then we drove the rest of the way back to the lake house in pensive silence. Every mile, every curve of the highway, every exit ramp and every car we passed seemed like an inevitable step toward my destiny. I felt a pull deep inside me to the lake that I had never felt before, not for a location or a person, or even for writing.

I rested my head against the window and watched as the landscape rolled by, knowing that I was less than an hour away from my life changing forever. The humidity outside was thick and oppressive and the air conditioning in Bianca's car was cold and oppressive. There was a thin layer of bubbly condensation though between the two zones that my cheek was resting on that gave me comfort and a sliver of refreshment. I didn't expect that the change my life was about to experience would be good but I hoped that somewhere between the hot and humid oppression of the heat of my crimes and the unrelenting cold air of the spirits haunting me, I could find the occasional pillow of condensation to rest my head on for comfort.

The throng of media was still camped out in the yard as we approached, but we were able to drive right by them without being swarmed. Once again, I was disappointed in how lazy they all were and wondered how many of them would kick themselves for missing the opportunity to speak to either of us once the dominoes started to fall when Jay and Cristal arrived—if they hadn't arrived already.

"Too bad we had to destroy the evidence," Bianca said as she pulled her car up to the main entrance, "because it would have been awesome to put Nelson's headless corpse up on the podium to answer questions like a creepier version of *Weekend at Bernie's*."

"Right, funny," I said, with little enthusiasm.

She tilted her head in confusion and gave me a weird look but didn't push the issue any further. I followed her inside and the minute we entered, I felt the atmosphere of the room change. Instead of the heat and humidity, I felt the cold of death, or approaching death. It was the same thing I had felt the last time I was at that house with Posey when her step-father-in-law summoned her to his quarters where he'd been hooked up to an array of life support devices. Could it be that Jay had taken a turn for the worst and was on death's doorstep?

I was surprised that thought didn't give me any comfort. I was more surprised the thought of being the one to pull the plug on Jay—or better yet, put a bullet in his head—didn't make me feel better either. The change I anticipated was beginning but it wasn't happening the way I expected. It didn't feel like payback or vengeance, it felt like...I don't know, I couldn't put my finger on it.

The whispers of death rattled inside my head and blasts of cold air raced by me from various directions. It felt like the air conditioner was malfunctioning, but it didn't seem to be affecting Bianca. She stayed in the living room to do what she could to prepare it for the press conference, but I knew the press conference wasn't going to happen and headed up toward the master bedroom where the strongest blast of air was coming from.

On my way up the curving staircase, the visions started. It started with Rickard then Posey then her brother, and finally Lindsey all circling me as I made my way up the stairs. The individual visions were followed by a faceless blur that swirled around my head, disorienting me and making me sick to my stomach. I swatted at the air, trying to break up the visions, but only succeeded in falling on my ass and rolling down three of the steps.

I knew then what I needed to do. My entire mission to that point had been one of payback, making other people atone for their sins against me and their sins against others. But it was only with the clarity that comes from exhaustion and air conditioning-induced visions that I realized it wasn't about payback, it was about concession. *I* was the guilty party. *I* needed to be judged. I needed to take that podium and answer for what I'd done, not tattle on what others had done.

Bianca tried to get my attention as I raced by her on my way through the living room toward the office. When I swung open the French doors to the office, I felt the biggest blast of cold air and knew that was where Parker had died. There was no sign of him ever having been there, but I could feel it. I guessed that Jay brought him back after finding him in our suite and tried to revive him. Whether it was because he cared about him or he wanted to keep him alive long enough to spill his secrets I didn't know. I sat down at the desk against the far wall so I was facing the doorway I'd just come through just in time to hear the first wave of violence. I knew there would be more violence, and I knew I'd survive it, but I didn't want to see it. The gun I'd been carrying was still in my pocket and I pulled it out and put it on the table next to me. I wanted to do what I'd always done when I had trouble making sense of the world: write.

Before I started writing though, I spun my chair around, pulled a decanter off of the small table next to the desk, and poured a small bit into a glass as the cracks of gunfire turned to the booms of shotgun. People were screaming now and I imagined the reporters were torn between fear for their lives and being part of the greatest stories of their careers. I drank the brown liquid down in one gulp. Bourbon. Good bourbon.

I heard the sounds of chaos getting closer as I finished up what I was writing, so I picked up the gun I had laid on the table next to my notepad. On the table, next to the letters, were a fountain pen and some fancy pencils I'd been meaning to try for almost the entire time I'd been a writer. I can't say I noticed any big difference between the fancy stuff and the cheap stick pens I normally worked with. Maybe the bourbon was making me less discerning.

The gun was loaded, but I checked again just to make sure. I'd read up as much as I could on where the best place was to hit for a quick, clean shot to juice the odds as much as I could in my favor. My legacy as a writer was set. My words were in the world and would live on after me. My legacy as a human disgusted me, but I was content that I'd done enough to end my curse. If I'd done what I was supposed to, it would all be over. If I'd missed something or done something wrong, I'd wake up as a vegetable or paralyzed or something horrible and unimaginable.

The final shot of bourbon was sweet and, for once in my life, I felt at ease with a decision I was making as I put the gun to my head.

I held it there long enough for my arm to start burning with tension but couldn't do it. Visions of Hemingway and any number of other legendary authors taken out in their prime gave me thoughts of legendary status, but I didn't have much in the way of work to establish that notoriety the more I thought about it. There was more work to be done.

Instead of a suicide note, I started writing down everything that had happened since I first ran into Posey

Wade outside of Parker Farmington's house and talked to her about kidnapping. It would serve double duty as my confession and as the outline for the stories I still had left to tell. Fiction hadn't worked out for me, but maybe I could make a career in non-fiction. I knew enough to secrets and dirt to keep myself off death row, but I knew I was staring down a long time behind bars. But right then, that didn't seem like such a bad thing.

I'd craved structure my entire life and maybe prison would give me that. I could turn my brain off and not worry about my life. Someone would tell me where to go and when to go there, that would leave my brain free to think about my stories. There were also still so many unanswered questions about what had been going on with Jay's business and Greg Herren's involvement, and whatever Martin Nelson's…Bill, had been up to. I hoped someone in that mess of reporters would have the initiative to take what I was about to give them and use it to connect the dots using their sources and fill in the blanks so I could read about it and know what happened.

I ran out of paper before I ran out of things to confess and had to dig around in the desk drawers to find extra paper. What I found instead made me smile and made me realize why I'd felt Parker's presence in that office. Mixed in with all the scrap paper and bills and invoices was a coffee-stained piece of paper that looked like a contract clipped to a stack of typewritten pages. I immediately recognized the stack of papers as my thesis and the form on top as the acceptance form Parker Farmington had refused to sign.

As far as I knew, Posey was the only one who ever had possession of that form after Parker gave it back to me and she must have kept it in this office. As I flipped through the pages though, refreshing my memory with how bad of a writer I'd been, I noticed some of the ink on the top form looked brighter than the rest. Below my signature and below the signature of my former department chair's was Parker's signature dated from last year.

When the gunfire died down, I made my way out to the porch and yelled for the media's attention. They swarmed around me and I could see a group of police officers approaching as well, so I spoke quickly.

"Have I got a story for you," I said.

ABOUT THE AUTHOR

BRYON QUERTERMOUS is the author of the Dominick Prince trilogy and the novel *Jackpot* with Stuart Woods. He lives in Michigan where he can be found screaming at the TV during football and baseball season and playing video games and board games with his kids the rest of the time. Visit him online at bryonquertermous.com and on Twitter @bryonq

On the following pages are a few
more great titles from the
Down & Out Books publishing family.

For a complete list of books and to
sign up for our newsletter,
go to DownAndOutBooks.com.

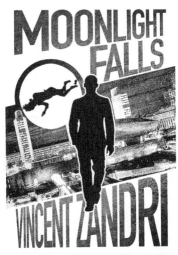

NEW YORK TIMES BESTSELLING AUTHOR

Moonlight Falls
A Dick Moonlight PI Thriller
Vincent Zandri

Down & Out Books
January 2021
978-1-64396-187-3

Albany, New York, is the dark setting of this paranoid thriller about Richard "Dick" Moonlight, former APD detective turned private investigator, who believes he killed Scarlet Montana—his illicit lover and wife of his ex-boss, Chief of Detectives Jake Montana. Problem is, despite the blood on his hands, Moonlight doesn't remember what happened!

Dark as Night
Mark T. Conard

Down & Out Books
February 2021
978-1-64396-179-8

Morris White is a Sous Chef at a first-rate Philadelphia French restaurant. All he wants is to leave behind his past—the poor neighborhood and petty crime he knew as a kid—and open his own restaurant.

The only thing that could stop them from turning their dream into a reality is Morris's half-brother, Vince, who is about to get out of Graterford Prison and is set on exacting revenge against the mobsters who ruined his life.

All Due Respect 2020
Chris Rhatigan & David Nemeth, editors

All Due Respect, an imprint of
Down & Out Books
November 2020
978-1-64396-165-1

Twelve short stories from the top writers in crime fiction today.

Featuring the work of Stephen D. Rogers, Tom Leins, Michael Pool, Andrew Davie, Sharon Diane King, Preston Lang, Jay Butkowski, Steven Berry, Craig Francis Coates, Bobby Mathews, Michael Penncavage, and BV Lawson.

White Trash and Dirty Dingoes
Jason Parent

Shotgun Honey, an imprint of
Down & Out Books
July 2020
978-1-64396-101-9

Gordon thought he'd found the girl of his dreams. But women like Sarah are tough to hang on to. When she causes the disappearance of a mob boss's priceless Chihuahua, she disappears herself, and the odds Gordon will see his lover again shrivel like nuts in a polar plunge.

With both money and love lost, he's going to have to kill some SOBs to get them back.

Made in the USA
Monee, IL
29 March 2021